Lord Stratford's new valet is hiding an outrageous secret!

Winston hung the gown on its usual peg. "If you will excuse me."

As she moved to walk past Lord Stratford, he grabbed her arm and held her still. His eyes widened even more when she looked up at him, and he gulped. "Winston?"

He knew. She was discovered. "Yes, my lord?"

His tongue darted out to wet his lips and she couldn't look away as he said, "Have you ever considered wearing a gown before?"

Desperately Seeking Seduction

HEATHER BOYD

Scandalous Brides Series
Book 1: Wicked With Him
Book 2: Desperately Seeking Seduction
Book 3: Love and Other Disasters

The characters and events portrayed in this book are fictitious.
Any similarity to real persons, living or dead, is purely
coincidental and not intended by the author.

DESPERATELY SEEKING SEDUCTION © 2023 by
Heather Boyd
Editing by Kelli Collins

Chapter One

L ord Stratford Sweet smirked. "It's big, isn't it?"

His companion turned obediently to look. "I've seen bigger."

"I'd like to know where," Stratford muttered, and then sat back with a grunt.

"It is impressive," Mr. Dane Winston offered with an indifferent shrug.

Stratford pursed his lips in annoyance at the faint praise for so grand a view. "Ravensworth Palace is one of the largest homes in all of England. You could get lost in there on the first day."

"I'll do my best not to," Winston murmured, a faint twist of condescension hovering on the fellow's lips. "But if I do, I will ask for directions, or perhaps a map."

Stratford had been forced to hire a replacement for his usual valet, Cuthbert, who'd been injured at the first inn they'd stopped at on his journey home. Cuthbert couldn't have carried out his duties with a broken wing and banged up head from his tumble down the staircase, and Stratford couldn't function without a valet to clean up after him. That way led to chaos and tardiness his brother the duke would tease him about. Although this fellow was young, Dane Winston had been eager to escape the inn where he'd been slaving away underpaid, for a better position and wages. Even if it was only to be a temporary position.

Winston was hard to figure out and harder to impress.

Stratford had taken him on despite only having the innkeepers word he was a sensible and dedicated worker and would give him no trouble. But as a traveling companion, he left a lot to be desired.

Winston's indifference to the things that mattered had begun to irk the longer they were trapped inside the slow-moving carriage. Stratford talked a lot, but Winston seemed to prefer their journey be conducted in near silence. It had already been an hour since their last real conversation. Stratford was about ready to toss Winston out to ride on the back of the carriage with the grooms. However, given the man's small stature, there was an obvious risk he'd lose the valet at any rough spot along the road.

He regarded Winston with a critical eye, yet again wondering if he'd made a mistake plucking him out for the plum role. Stratford was the younger brother of the new Duke of Ravenswood, after all. But given that Winston had performed all the duties expected of a valet exceptionally well —save for conversation—he had little choice but to keep him until Cuthbert recovered and appeared at Ravenswood Palace. If only Winston had a more outgoing personality, Stratford would be entirely satisfied with his new employee.

He sighed and set his preoccupation for getting a rise out of his new employee aside until later. Coming home would be interesting. It was the first time he'd ever looked forward to it, that he could ever remember. The long-suffering servants should be happy about it too. "You can trust the butler to set you right. That man knows every nook and cranny in the place. He rose through the ranks from pot boy. As for the other servants, I could not say who you might rely upon."

Winston nodded. "I will be guided by your wisdom."

"That would be a nice change. I told Cuthbert to watch that step and he still blundered into a fall," Stratford complained. "Cuthbert surely must have noticed the wobble going up."

But on the trip down the next morning, he took a tumble and had broken bone. Quite an unsettling howl he'd made, too. By midday, Stratford had known he had to leave the moaning servant behind. It was not every day your beloved elder brother hosted the family for the first time since becoming the Duke of Ravenswood. Stratford was already late.

He turned to take in the view of his ancestral home as they drew nearer. Ravenswood Palace, deep in the heart of Somerset, was a truly spectacular building. Four floors in total, thirty-five bedchambers. Nestled on a slight rise of land. It commanded a view of many miles in every direction.

But best of all was what would be found inside. He could not wait to see all those smug faces in the family wiped clean when they were denied the privilege of the new duke's favor. Their hands outstretched and smiles imploring, and then those same greedy hands closing over nothing but air as their smiles became a mere memory. It was their own damn fault that Ravenswood would never give any one of them a penny. They should have been kinder to him all along, rather than pandering to the late Duke of Ravenswood's capricious whims because he preferred to foster competitiveness for his attention.

Stratford's elder brother, Algernon Sweet, sixth Duke of Ravenswood, did not suffer fools. And the family had a legion of those. He would have to be on his guard, and Stratford had counted on Cuthbert keeping his ear to the ground in the servants' hall for any potential signs of trouble. Without Cuthbert's insights, he would have to face the family at large with more of a disadvantage than usual.

But Stratford had made the best of a bad situation. The inn really had only the one decent footman who had dared apply for the position before Stratford had decided he even had need of a replacement. Mr. Dane Winston had seemed the only logical choice. Quite bold, too. He'd quickly gathered up Stratford's things strewn about the room, spoke with his moaning valet, and promised Stratford would not regret his hire.

And he had not, for the first days, but he would wait to pass judgement until he'd spent a few days at Ravenswood. That would surely be a test of his new valet's mettle.

When the carriage finally stopped at the front of Ravenswood Palace, he bounded out and rushed toward the massive carved old entrance doors, leaving the servants to do what they normally did when he wasn't around. It was not strictly a palace, Ravenswood, but the name had stuck, and Father of course would never have diminished the family's importance by changing it back to merely calling it an overly large manor house.

The Ravenswood butler stepped out the doors before he could reach them, beaming a smile of welcome. "Lord Stratford. Welcome home."

Stratford handed him his hat and gloves immediately. "Good to see you, Seymour. My usual valet fell ill along the way." Stratford turned to see Winston scrambling out of the carriage. "That fellow has taken Cuthbert's place temporarily. He'll explain it all. Where is the duke and my brothers?"

Seymour nodded. "The duke is in his study,

my lord. I believe your brothers are with His Grace there, too."

"Good."

Stratford hurried inside, his boots ringing upon the marble entrance floor, and headed toward the ducal study, keen to be reunited with his elder siblings and hear the latest ondit.

Algernon Sweet, Duke of Ravenswood, clad all in black, stood with his back to Stratford when he rushed into the room, looking out upon the lawn that was now his own, but Nash and Jasper faced the door. They saw Stratford and burst to their feet.

"My apologies for being the last to arrive," he said in a rush.

"Trouble?" Jasper asked, coming closer to embrace him. Jasper was just a year older than Stratford, but far wiser...and a worse rogue than them all combined.

"Only that my valet fell a day out of London. I had to leave him behind to recover his health and composure."

"I'll loan you mine," offered Nash, the second eldest, holding out his hand to shake.

"Not necessary. I found a replacement at the inn." Stratford ignored the hand and embraced his brother. Nash, as usual, was stiff and unyielding and their embrace was awkward and brief. He didn't know why he continued to hug his second-eldest brother. He'd simply always tried to breach his reserve, and usually failed to close the distance between them.

He turned his attention to Algernon, the eldest of them all, who had finally turned, and Stratford bowed deeply and theatrically to the new duke. "Your Grace. It is a pleasure to see you again."

Ravenswood stepped close, looking down at him with a scowl from his greater height. "You're not quite the last to arrive for the gathering," Ravenswood chided, but then ruined the complaint by suddenly scuffing up Stratford's hair, as he'd always done when Stratford was younger. He stepped back with a laugh before Stratford could attempt to retaliate. "You'll need better wits about you today," Ravenswood warned.

Stratford rushed to straighten his hair again, grinning and pleased that inheriting a lofty title of duke had not affected their bond yet. It was nice to be around family who cared about him. Algernon always had been his favorite brother. "Who are we waiting for?"

"You'll see in due time. But first…" He gave a signal to his other brothers and as one, they closed and locked the study doors and windows, keeping everyone out. "Since you are the last brother to arrive, you are unfortunately the last to know."

Stratford stilled. "Know what?"

Ravenswood threw his arms wide, clearly agitated. "That the estate is in a bloody shambles. Not a penny to spare anywhere!"

Nash hurried to their brother's side and placed a restraining hand on the new duke's chest before he could make a further loud outburst. "Calm yourself, Ravenswood."

"I am trying," the duke said through gritted teeth.

Stratford shook his head and looked about. Everything that he'd seen since his arrival was exactly the same as when their father had lived. "That's not possible."

"He wasted it all," Ravenswood growled softly. "Bastard left me with empty accounts and a mountain of debt plus the inevitable embarrassment of trying to pay it back."

Stratford glanced at his brothers, seeking their reactions. Neither looked shocked by the news now. Though they'd probably had time to calm themselves, unlike Stratford. He struggled to believe it. They had all believed the estate would go on as it always had, just with a kinder duke at the helm. The reading of the will had not alluded to any particular problems for the estate. But the running of the Ravenswood duchy was a costly enterprise.

And now there was no money to pay for anything.

Stratford glanced at Ravenswood again and feared for his favorite brother. "What will you do?"

Ravenswood exhaled loudly, and Nash moved

away from the duke. "What I must before the news breaks and the laughter starts."

Stratford's eyes rounded, and he looked to the windows and imagined the awkwardness of meeting his entire family shortly, hiding the burden of a mountain of debt. "Does anyone suspect yet? The cousins and uncles and aunts beyond us four, I mean."

"We sincerely hope they do not," Jasper murmured, clapping a hand on Stratford's shoulder.

Stratford took in his brothers' worried faces and gulped. He was the youngest, but he was one of them. A Sweet. And loyal to his elder brothers and their ambitions. "Well, I'm not going to tell anyone."

"We never imagined you would," Nash murmured, coming up on his other side. "It is vital we all pretend everything is as expected for the duration of the family gathering and for as long as possible beyond."

Stratford agreed. For years, they had all danced to their father's tune, waiting for this moment to arrive when they would be free. Even though they were all the duke's legitimate sons and heirs, other parts of the family had been treated far better. And to make matters worse, the late duke had encouraged that family friction and enjoyed their small squabbles. He'd had his favorites, and had always sided with them against his own grown sons. All in an effort to prove his power. To make them toe his line or risk being cast out of the will.

Those favored relations would enjoy their embarrassment when the news of the state of their financial affairs became known. Rub the loss in their noses. Ravenswood, particularly, would be placed in an awkward position. He had gained a title but an empty one.

He might be forever in debt.

Stratford had always believed that upon the duke's death, things would improve with Algernon as the head of the family. That they would all have the upper hand for once and live peacefully. But they would likely only have more trouble than before with this development.

Stratford took in his eldest brother's face and noticed the tightness of his jaw and high color upon his cheeks. Algernon was understandably humiliated by this turn of events.

Stratford gulped when Nash made an effort to check the duke's heart by grabbing his wrist to feel for the pulse. Nash would have been an excellent physician in the family if father had let him go for a proper career. As it was, he had only studied in secret, practicing his doctoring on his brothers and their willing servants. He was utterly devoted to Algernon's continued good health and happiness, wishing fervently that nothing stand in the way of their elder brother's inheritance. Nash would be watching him very closely, now he was duke. They all would be.

"What can I do?" he whispered.

Nash nodded, leaving the duke be at last. "We have, Jasper and I, given over our entire fortunes to our eldest brother in an effort to keep the estate running smoothly, but even that is not going to be enough."

Jasper and Nash stared at him, but Ravenswood glanced away, no doubt embarrassed by their generosity. Ravenswood had always helped them. Paying off any small debts incurred beyond their quarterly allowance from his own pocket so father might never know.

Stratford shuffled his feet, knowing what was being asked of him without it being said out loud. While he wanted to help his eldest brother, what he had saved himself in the last years was not very much at all. He'd never been good at keeping track of where his money went. And it seemed to have slipped through his fingers like water in recent years for one reason or another while living in London. He ought to have paid more attention to his finances.

But Algernon was his brother and the head of the family now. The man who'd essentially raised him, ensured he was well cared for all his life. Educated him, too, and Stratford had always been clothed in Algernon's finest castoffs. Father and Mother had not given a damn about their two younger sons, other than receiving regular reports that he and Jasper were still breathing. All their care and attention had gone to Algernon and

Nash, the heir and spare. But that had only been to a point, as well.

He caught his elder brother's eye. "It's not much but you can have what I possess."

His other brothers exhaled. "So, it's settled. We'll sell Freemont Villa, and Highland Cottage, and now Clifford Lodge, along with those cottages you purchased from Barnes recently. That should bring in a tidy sum to keep the worst of the debtors at bay."

Stratford raked a hand through his hair and winced. Clifford Lodge had only just become his, a bequest in his late father's will. He'd spent less than a week there himself since Father's passing. He had planned to go back soon. Now he no longer could. But then again, Nash and Jasper had inherited Highland Cottage and Freemont Villa, respectively, and they were giving them up as well, so he shouldn't complain. He wasn't the only one losing out in all of this.

"Thank you, but know you won't remain empty-handed," Ravenswood murmured to him quietly. "Nash has drawn up a plan of attack and there are contracts between us to be signed. You will receive surplus profits from the ducal estate annually until the value of your sold property is reached, and for three years beyond that. You should end up richer than you are now."

"But where will I live?"

"You will stay here or at Ravenswood House in London."

"Surely you don't want me living with you," he said, laughing awkwardly. Stratford loved his older brothers, but he also knew he often annoyed them, too. He talked a lot and was somewhat forgetful. Nash was always with the duke, and he had a particularly short fuse for interruptions and conversation.

"Father may not have wanted us about, but I want my brothers near," Ravenswood promised. "You will all stay with me. I couldn't take your money any other way. You will have the advantage of having this duke's ear, for what it's worth."

Jasper caught Stratford's eye and grinned widely. "He's not that fond of us. He just doesn't want to be left to deal with the family rabble all on his own when they come banging on his door."

When Ravenswood's lips twitched, indicating unspoken agreement with Jasper's sentiment, Stratford felt a smile forming on his face, too. None of them wanted that, but it had always been easier to deal with the family together. "Our cousins and uncles and aunts are accustomed to preferential treatment."

"They are about to get a rude shock," Nash murmured. "Our new duke will have a reputation as a taciturn penny-pincher."

"The howls of outrage will be loud when they realize they'll have to pay their own bills," Jasper whispered. "And we will have the front-row seats to witness their many hardships."

Stratford rubbed his hands together and laughed. "This is going to be such fun."

"Don't get carried away," Nash warned. "Tread lightly for now. You can break out into song when we have him married."

Stratford swiveled to stare at Algernon. His elder brother looked decidedly uncomfortable at the announcement of a wedding for himself. "No!"

"Yes," Ravenswood murmured. "Father has given me no choice but to marry a woman for her money. He couldn't get me to wed his choice while he was alive. In death, the bastard might get his black heart's desire."

They would all be miserable if Algernon had to marry Lady Stephanie Kent, the heiress father had favored all along. A colder woman could not be found anywhere in England. She had pots of money, pride to match, and wished with every breath to become the next Duchess of Ravenswood.

So did Algernon's current mistress, Lady Barnes, although she was already married.

The two women hated each other.

Stratford winced thinking of Algernon's future, caught between a wife and a mistress. There would be fireworks when they returned to London.

And they would all have to answer to a duchess one day. Live together in the same house for years, too, until their loans were repaid in full.

Stratford was not looking forward to that future. It would be a nightmare he'd wish on no one.

There was a tap on the door, and Jasper rushed to answer it.

But it was only the butler. "A carriage approaches, Your Grace. I believe it is the one you are waiting for."

Ravenswood nodded. "Bring her to me immediately."

Stratford winced. Dear God. Was it so bad that Ravenswood meant to announce he would marry that very day? "Should we leave you to it?"

Jasper slapped his shoulder. "It's not what you think."

"Then what is it?" His brothers all grinned, and he scowled at them. "Why am I the last to know anything in this family?"

"You should have been the very first." Algernon brushed at his dark sleeve and turned away. "He was your friend, after all."

Stratford frowned at him. "What friend?"

"Wait and see," Ravenswood murmured, taking up a position at the window with his back to the door, as he'd been standing when Stratford had arrived.

A few minutes later, footsteps could be heard coming toward the study, and he turned to see his recently scandalous cousin, Amity Sweet, a woman not seen in many months, sweep into the room on the arm of his best friend, Roman Crawford.

Stratford blinked in surprise to see them

together—and then his eyes narrowed in suspicion. Amity had ruined herself earlier that year without naming the scoundrel who'd done it.

So, there was no reason for that pair to be together. Unless…

Chapter Two

Interrogations came in many forms. This first one was perhaps the most important for a new valet. Winston let the curtain fall over the view of the expansive grounds of Ravenswood Palace and turned to face the bedchamber again. "I've been in service all my life, sir," Winston told Mr. Seymour, the Ravenswood butler, who was hovering and watching as Lord Stratford's trunks were carefully deposited in the chamber by the footmen.

There were twelve trunks in total. Winston had never known any male traveler to carry so many trunks before, and could not wait to unpack the contents to find out what they contained. Fine clothing was Winston's weakness, and Lord Stratford dressed very well indeed.

Unpacking would have to wait until the butler had gone, though. The older man had first watched from the far doorway until beckoned inside. Winston knew better than to put off the inevitable questions about replacing Cuthbert so abruptly. Butlers were the most important men in any household, and this one had been asking questions for five minutes already.

"I came here as a boy and never left," the older

man murmured, leaning against the bedpost momentarily.

Winston was not surprised by the butler's admission. Some servants were as immovable as the vast homes they served. They often had limited patience for outsiders, too. Cuthbert had said he'd come from London, and so far, he didn't seem unduly missed by any servant here.

"Never, sir?" Winston approached the only trunk opened during the journey and took out a nightshirt and laid it across the high pillows already on the bed, along with Stratford's silk robe. Not that there was much hope the man might choose to wear either garment. He hadn't so far after Winston's three days in his service. But Lord Stratford carried them, and the option was there for him to don either garment should he ever choose to be modest.

"No. I never wanted more for my life than this," he said. "My family is here, in the village two miles away. I see them once or twice a year," he admitted.

"The first butler I ever worked with was much the same," Winston promised, closing one trunk and opening the next, nearly crowing at the excitement of seeing a fine dark navy-blue cloth—perhaps a frock coat—on top. "He was devoted to his post and the family he had worked for all his life, much like you."

The butler approached. "Why did you leave that post?"

"I wasn't wanted," Winston said with a shrug and picked up the coat, frowning. It would need pressing before it could be worn. Lord Stratford could not wear wrinkled garments. Cuthbert should have packed this trunk far better than he had. "And I wanted to see something of the world, sir."

The old butler scoffed at the idea. "And was it all you expected?"

"Yes, and no."

"That is the case with everything. When you are older, you'll understand the world can be wherever you find yourself, and you should be grateful to belong anywhere," the butler said condescendingly.

Winston didn't want to belong. Never had. Never would. Although, Winston would give anything to belong to a coat like this one. When the butler was gone, Winston would properly unpack and admire everything normally beyond the reach of a mere servant.

Winston glanced at the easel propped up against the bed, then cast an eye about the room, looking for the best place to move it to. Lord Stratford claimed to be something of an artist, but he had given no directions for the easel's positioning.

Mr. Seymour approached. "Move that chair, set the easel at an angle facing the bed. Lord Stratford paints in the mornings. The light is best then, he says."

"Thank you, sir," Winston murmured before grasping a large, heavy armchair single-handedly and maneuvering it out of the way. "My predecessor gave no instructions for that stack of paintings, either."

The butler started to flick through them. There were more than a dozen to go through. Some complete, others painted over in one color as if he had been unhappy with the work and wanted to hide it. "Lord Stratford keeps them anywhere about the room he likes until he's no wish to see them anymore. Then they are stored in the attics, with all the others he's painted over the years."

"Are there many?"

"Dozens, I should imagine. Only a few were deemed good enough to have been hung about the palace. The late duke…" The older man did not finish his statement, but he didn't really have to. Winston could well imagine a powerful duke would have no time for what might be considered a younger son's frivolous pastime. He wondered briefly how Lord Stratford stood in the current duke's eyes. He was a younger brother and might be considered a burden on the estate, as many were.

Winston grappled with one large unfinished work, carefully set it on the easel, and then stood back. "This is, I believe, his latest work."

The butler came around the easel to view it. "Unfinished."

"Indeed."

Lord Stratford had spent most of the evenings of the journey staring at it, but had not painted even a single brushstroke on the canvas. It was of a voluptuous woman reclining on pillows in a flowing red gown, surrounded by candles. She was very beautiful. Why else paint her, of course? Perhaps she was his sweetheart or lover or even his own wife. Lord Stratford had never said he was married, and Winston had not thought to ask. But it was easy to see what the painting might become if the young lord spent more time finishing the canvas, and less trying to provoke a rise out of his temporary valet. He had talked constantly about his home, and pestered Winston with questions, too.

And once they'd arrived, he had immediately run off to meet his brothers without so much as a backward glance. Winston couldn't ever imagine feeling that same way about going home.

Home was a place where she didn't belong.

Home was where she had been exposed as a fraud.

Dane Winston was as much a figment of her imagination as the name she'd been christened with by her parents. Once, Winston had lived as the sole male heir to a wealthy man's fortune. None but her scheming mother and a few trusted servants had ever known the truth until the end.

The discovery of Winston's true gender had

come as the rudest of shocks to her up-till-then proud father.

Winston continued to dress the part of a man now, in order to make her way in the world.

Gaining a valet's position with Lord Stratford was an unlooked-for boon Winston could not afford to waste. She didn't know how to live as a woman, and the money from the generous wage she'd be paid would go a long way in her needy hands.

With a nod to the butler, she continued the unpacking. She knew enough of the workings of a great house to know to be silent and unobtrusive at all times. No one but the servants should have reason to look at her twice.

And even then, as valet, she held an important position in this household. Her past should not be questioned too closely by others of lesser rank. She would enjoy the luxury of having a chamber of her own, too, and being a step removed from almost everyone born male in service. Winston would never become friends with anyone here. Her service to Lord Stratford would be short. But to the butler, she would extend every consideration and convey the utmost respect.

"The family takes meals together for luncheon and again at eight o'clock in the evening for supper. By family, I refer to His Grace the Duke of Ravenswood, his brothers Lord Nash, Lord Jasper and your employer, Lord Stratford. It is important that Lord Stratford arrives promptly at mealtimes.

He can be tardy when he becomes too absorbed in his art."

"I will keep that in mind, and should he linger too long, remind him if need be."

"See that you do. Meals are served in the servants' hall at nine in the morning, two in the afternoon and ten in the evening unless there is a ball, when it will be served much later. If you miss a meal, you will have to await the next one. We will all be much too busy to worry about your whereabout in the coming days."

"Yes, of course." Winston had hardly had a decent meal at the inn where she'd last been employed, and could scarcely imagine going hungry here.

"Bathing is conducted twice a week by precedent, in the facilities the late duke built especially for the servants to use. You will be fifth in the line, and you must be quick about it. Again, should you miss your turn, you will have to wait till the next day. There is no bathing upstairs by any servant, in any bedchamber. The copper tubs are reserved for members of the family or guests. Infractions will lead to instant dismissal."

"I understand," she promised. Discovery was always her greatest fear, and she did not undress in front of others. She would have to become very clever regarding how she went about washing while she was here. She nodded to the butler. "Is there anything else I should know?"

"Yes, due to the house party guests bringing a

greater number of servants than expected, you will have to sleep in Lord Stratford's closet, upon the floor, for the first few nights."

She nodded again but was disappointed. It meant she might be around her employer a great deal more than she'd planned to. But Winston had slept on the floor before, and in far worse places. The closet was as spacious as the last inn's main guest chamber, and it did appear to have a lock on the inside of the door. It would only be for a few nights anyway. And when Cuthbert returned, whenever that might be, she would be on her way to a new place of employment.

Sleeping in a dressing closet did mean that she might never be alone at night around other men, besides Lord Stratford. That was to her advantage. The fewer people who looked at her jaw, the better. "Very good, sir."

"I'm sure you'll pick up enough of the ways of the palace to manage until Cuthbert arrives. If I could give you one piece of advice—do not get too comfortable."

"I will do my best to remember that," she promised.

The old fellow strode from the room and shut the door quietly behind him.

Winston exhaled and relaxed a little, glad to finally be alone for the first time in hours. She rubbed her face hard. She hadn't dared let down her guard all day to smile. But she had never been truly comfortable anywhere she'd lived, so she could do this. Fool them all yet again. It was not as if she didn't know how demanding wealthy gentlemen could be toward their servants. If she kept busy, did her work to the highest standard possible, she'd be well-rewarded when it came time to be on her merry way.

The world was rife for opportunities of employment for someone like her. Someone efficient but forgettable. And if she did not please her employer, there was always the next town, next county, and a new name with which to begin again. She'd kept moving since her ruse had been discovered, never stopping in one place too long for fear of what might be coming after her.

Winston was aware that her fears might have been somewhat paranoid, but she suspected her father might well remember he'd once had a son who had really been a daughter in disguise. She had played her part and deceived him, along with everyone else. Papa had been furious with her. He'd been made a fool.

Poor Papa.

It hadn't been her decision to lie to her father about her real gender. The lie had been told since the moment of her birth by a woman craftier and more devious and unscrupulous than anyone she'd ever met since.

Mama.

Winston shrugged and turned back to the

unfinished portrait and stared at it blindly until the unproductive guilt and anger passed, and then contemplated the painting's subject. Winston knew more about the world, art, than she liked to let on. Lord Stratford definitely had talent. She wasn't sure yet what else he was good for, though, except blather.

Winston's father had given her every advantage as his sole heir, the best education, the best clothing, until she'd been found out and ended up with nothing but the clothes she'd stood up in. She shook her head and strode over to the window and took in the view once more, gnawing on her lower lip in regret over things she could not change.

Outside, she could see people—the Sweet family, she assumed—milling about on the neatly clipped lawn under the late spring sunshine. The well-dressed gentlemen, and their fashionably attired wives and daughters, drank from delicate crystal glasses and ate off fine white China plates. Musicians played a merry tune that carried even as far as this room. Those women in beautiful clothing and jewels were fluttering their fans, trying to attract the attention of men, and laughing merrily.

Mother had been just like them. Fawning over Father and lying to his face every single day since Winston had been born. All Mama had cared about was her ambition to get her hands on more of his money, relish the prestige of being a rich man's wife, and equally determined to keep utter control over Winston's future. She'd made a mockery of Winston's entire existence with a pretty smile on her lips all the while, and little regard for honesty.

Winston was more interested in the gentlemen, their actions, and the way they carried on around each other. She studied men in order to emulate their behavior.

Her gaze caught on her employer, standing slightly back from the others gathered below her. Lord Stratford was handsome, as many young lords often were, and he had excellent taste in clothes. She'd seen enough of passing travelers to notice how he was different. He watched others, similar to the way she always did, but he talked far too much to a servant whose opinion shouldn't ever be asked for so often.

Unfortunately, there was something odd about Lord Stratford that she couldn't quite put her finger on. From their first encounter on the stairs at the inn, the night before the valet Cuthbert had taken his fall, she'd found him…familiar. And not in a good way. She'd not truly liked him on sight, believing him indolent and spoiled upon first hearing one of his many rambling speeches to his valet. But aside from his constant blather, she had no clear reason to have taken such an immediate set against him.

Yet, once the valet had fallen afoul of the stairs, she'd seen another side of the man. The goodness. The consideration and kindness he'd shown for the injured valet was far and away more than most employers ever showed for a servant's welfare at such a time. Lord Stratford had sat with the valet as his broken arm had been set, feeding him liquor from his own luggage to numb the pain, and talking to him to distract him from the doctor's work.

And his reluctance to leave the poor fellow behind, warring with his need to be on his way, had been palpable, and the reason she'd finally approached him to offer her services as a temporary replacement until Cuthbert could resume his duties.

She could not have stayed too much longer at the inn and hope to escape detection anyway. The innkeeper kept wanting to get drunk with her, and when he did, he tended to forget his amorous inclinations were not welcomed by a supposedly male servant.

Winston noticed Lord Stratford glance up at the house—and it seemed he was looking directly at her. She quickly stepped farther back from the window, lest it seem she was shirking her new duties as his new valet. It wouldn't do to appear lazy in front of the man who would pay her the generous wages he'd promised. Tomorrow was soon enough to get the lay of the land outside, but today was for learning how to navigate the house so she could avoid crossing paths with anyone who might look too closely at her face.

Winston brushed her fingers over her smooth jaw, cursing her gender yet again, and turned to the fireplace. She scraped her fingers through the soot and went to the mirror to apply a small amount to her smooth jaw and un-whiskered upper lip. Her skin was the only thing about her that was soft. The rest of her was strong. She'd built muscles by boxing alone in her chambers, keeping up the training begun in childhood, so she could tote luggage at the inn.

She was alone in the world. She would fight anyone who dared try to take advantage of her small stature, or her gender, should it be discovered. Over the years, she'd hardened her heart never to care about anyone she'd met, too, no matter how kindly disposed they might have been to her in the beginning. It had been ages since she'd let her guard down, and she vowed she never would again.

Satisfied with the slightest darkening of her jaw from the soot, a mere hint of stubble to be shaved later, she prowled the room, stoking the fire and fluffing all the pillows on the bed. Lord Stratford would return to his bedchamber to change before dinner. She had to prepare for that. To finish the unpacking. To shave him, comb his long soft hair, dress him in his fine clothes without touching him, and make sure he was not at all late.

She would not waste this opportunity. A fine home like this, a duke's residence, would also house a most interesting library. There, she might for the first time in a decade do a little digging into her own family. It would be nice to not look over her shoulder constantly, always wondering if her father was still alive and looking for her still.

Chapter Three

"I thought Uncle Henry would never stop talking tonight," Stratford said by way of apology as he entered the duke's study late in the evening after supper. It had been a long and annoying day, for all of them. The family members were relentless in their pursuit of winning the duke's favor, and his ear for a quiet word or ten. Stratford had even physically put himself between Algernon and the worst of the shameless hussies they called cousins. Each woman eager to catch the duke's eye and win herself a husband in him. Algernon would never marry a cousin, much less a poor cousin such as they all were.

He noted two of his brothers leaning over the ducal desk with serious expressions on display. "What's to do now?"

"We've been strategizing again," Jasper murmured with a tired smile as he left the desk to sit down, nursing a glass of brandy in his hand.

Nash removed his spectacles, his expression grim as he polished them on a cloth. "We have to decide who the duke will set his cap for."

Stratford glanced around for his eldest brother and found him reclining on a long couch near the fire, nearly out of sight, legs crossed at the ankles and one dark-clad arm thrown casually over his eyes. "Truly?"

"The decision could have waited until tomorrow, surely," Ravenswood murmured without looking at Stratford. "Thanks to you all, I have a year to decide on an alternate bride."

"A year at most, brother," Nash warned. "The quicker it's done, the better. For us, too."

Ravenswood sat up at the softly spoken rebuke. "Yes, of course. I cannot have you put your lives on hold forever."

"We don't mind," Stratford murmured. He and Jasper had talked a little during the surprise wedding celebrations for their cousin Amity and his best friend Crawford. It was bound to be a rough few years ahead. Their elder brother hated that he needed their help, let alone taking money from them all. It had not been his idea, but he couldn't refuse such a gift. Nash had decided on his own to hand over his fortune and hatched a plan to support the duke until the estate was turning a profit. Jasper had taken a day or two to decide it was a good idea, too. "What help can we be, though?"

"Other than moral support?" Ravenswood asked.

"Being married isn't that much of a chore," Nash murmured.

They all turned to look at him. Only Nash was married. Had two young sons upstairs in the nursery somewhere, but no one had seen his bride,

Laura, since just after the birth of the second son. She'd had enough of the family and run away.

Ravenswood stood and drew close to Nash and asked the question Stratford had pondered from time to time. "Do you even know she's still alive?"

Nash frowned and looked away.

Stratford winced and looked away, too, as an awkward silence descended over them all. There was no love lost between Nash and Laura. He'd married her for her money years ago, and she'd known it. As soon as she'd done her duty and delivered up two healthy sons, she'd escaped her husband and the suffocating life they'd all endured under their late father's tight rules and endless interference. As far as Stratford knew, Nash had not even tried to bring her back.

The rest of them had, at the time, no choice but to stay, of course. "So, who do you favor?" Stratford asked, changing the subject back to Algernon's problems as he strolled toward the ducal desk.

Ledgers were spread across the usually clean surface. A piece of paper topped each one. Each note was scrawled with an amount in Nash's hand or corrected by the duke's. Five thousand pounds on one. Twelve thousand pound on another. Each ledger detailing yet more debt than the last until Stratford's knees grew weak. "Dear God," he whispered. "It's worse than you made out."

"Any wonder Ravenswood is not sleeping anymore."

"The stuff of nightmares," Stratford agreed, nodding.

"So, to business," Nash said briskly. "Jasper, quickly check the hall for Cousin George again. He's been trailing after the duke and trying to get a private interview with him all day."

Jasper checked and came back grinning. "All clear."

"The most money to be found is with either the Wellington, Fairbridge or Knox families."

Stratford squinted, recalling the members of those families. "Only three women of suitable age to choose from among them. That's a short list."

"The duke requires a bride equal to the honor of becoming his duchess, too. Only the best will do," Nash assured them with a tight smile.

"Monied is all that really matters in the end," Ravenswood countered. "There may be others who've fallen out of favor with society. Tell me anyone else you younger two can think of with a dowry nearing fifty-thousand pounds."

Stratford mentioned any heiress he could remember having met but most were dowered much lower than needed. Jasper did the same. Between them, they added three more names for the duke's consideration. Six was not a lot to choose from, either. Stratford did not envy his eldest brother. "Does that help?"

"Possibly," Ravenswood remarked, grimacing

and gesturing to the ledgers across his desk. "Now to the debts. Mr. Aston is owed a significant sum."

"If only he had a daughter to marry to reduce the debt. Let us hope he might have forgotten about the money owed to him," Jasper murmured.

"If he'd had a daughter, we'd have heard about it already," the duke said dryly. "But I wouldn't count on any surprise offspring from him given the fraught state of his marriage in recent years."

Between them, they racked their brains to settle on a short list of who they thought might be the next richest heiresses in England. When the duke dismissed them to their beds, he asked Stratford to remain behind.

Algernon winced as soon as the others were gone. "Not the triumphant homecoming I'd planned for you all to enjoy," he said by way of apology.

"No, I suppose not but at least I had the joy of watching Cousin George's face when you introduced Mr. and Mrs. Crawford on the lawn today."

Ravenswood laughed softly. "Yes, that was a definite high point of the day, seeing him nearly frothing at the mouth like the dog he is. He can do nothing about it now."

"Crawford should have told me he fancied her," Stratford complained. "Had I known it was him that ruined her, I would have said something."

Ravenswood put a restraining hand on his

arm. "Crawford would have been shot. George already hated him."

"The feeling is mutual, I'm sure."

"Yes. Cousin Amity saved herself an unpleasant marriage that night, and we can be thankful she's now married to a rich man she seems to love. At least I don't have to worry for her future."

He caught a hint of wistfulness in the duke's tone. A love match was not on the cards for his elder brother or for Stratford either. "I'm sorry about all this, brother."

Algernon nodded. "As am I. Listen, I can do without that little country house you love. I know you were looking forward to escaping there to paint."

"Sweet men keep their promises no matter what," he insisted. "Are you going to deny me my art while I live here, like father tried to do?"

"Why would I do that? Where else might I commission the expected portrait of myself without incurring another blasted debt?" he said, wearing a weary grin.

"I'll hold you to that," Stratford warned but was pleased as punch he was first choice for the artist to paint the newly anointed duke. He'd painted his brothers many times before and looked forward to making this brother appear more regal than he already was. But he also understood he was only getting the commission because he'd work for free. "At present, I have a commission to finish. I've sketched Lady Newport any number of times, however, her husband requires a much larger canvas done."

Algernon sighed. "So, you will not be staying with us for long then?"

"You do not get rid of me that easily, brother," he said, laughing. "I'm doing the work here and sending word to Newport to come fetch it. That had already been discussed and agreed upon since before I heard Father had died."

Ravenswood groaned and plucked at his black waistcoat. "I thought his death would make my life easier."

Stratford patted his shoulder. "It will be. One day soon, I promise."

"Forever the optimist, little brother," Ravenswood complained, messing up Stratford's hair again.

He managed to retaliate that time. He laughed at the duke as he danced backward to avoid a playful fight erupting between them. "Well, think of it this way. If you didn't exist, George might have inherited."

The new duke shot him a sour look. "Over my dead body."

"And ours, too." He pulled a face. "Someone might notice a killing spree on that scale."

The duke grunted.

"You look tired. You should get some sleep."

"You ought to go up to bed, too. Tomorrow

will be another exhausting day tiptoeing around the subject of funds and favors."

"Yes, I should see if my new valet is settled in or completely lost somewhere about the house."

"If he's not any good as a valet, let me know and you can borrow Dobb."

"The new fellow is competent so far. But it has only been a few days, so... I will let you know later if I need Dobb or Nash's man to step in."

"Good. Thank you again, Stratford."

He bowed deeply to his brother. "You are welcome, Duke."

Ravenswood laughed and shooed him away. "Sleep well."

Stratford strolled to the door and let himself out. He was not three yards away from the ducal study when Cousin George called out to him from down the hall.

"Care for a nightcap, cousin?"

He turned to study his older cousin, the bully of the family, noting the flush of his cheeks and the glaze of his eyes. The man had been drinking hard all day and it was never very pleasant to encounter him at any hour on such a night. "Perhaps another time."

Stratford turned for the stairs.

"You think you've got the upper hand now, don't you? Think you've got it all."

Stratford paused on the stairs. "Was there a contest I missed between us?"

"My sister. That was your doing. You and your

wretched friend conspired to see my side thoroughly embarrassed! You used your own cousin to do it, too."

Stratford shook his head. "Didn't have to lift a finger myself. Amity has her own mind, and you embarrass yourself with no help from anyone on my side of the family."

"Why, you little toad! I ought to teach you a lesson in—"

"You will teach my brother nothing," Ravenswood warned in an ominous tone that made Cousin George spin about, looking for the duke. Ravenswood appeared from the shadows slowly, glowering at their drunken cousin. There was no love lost between the pair. They'd been enemies for a very long time for no reason other than Algernon had been the late duke's firstborn son. "If you know what is good for you, Mr. Sweet, you will cease all harassment of my younger brother and take yourself to bed. Continue, and you and your branch of the family will suffer the consequences of my displeasure."

Stratford shivered. When he wanted to be, Ravenswood could sound as ruthless as their father had always been. Only his brothers knew the kindness of his private heart.

George cast the duke a belligerent glare and then marched up the stairs ahead of Stratford.

"Watch your back with him," Stratford warned his eldest brother.

"Better watch yours, too," Ravenswood

suggested, frowning after their cousin. "He's more like our father than I care for."

"I'll keep that in mind," Stratford promised, but he'd always known not to trust that particular cousin, and his own father as well.

He went up the stairs slowly, checking every corner where George might linger to accost him again. But he entered the family wing without incident, passing a pair of footmen stationed in the hallway. Their presence ensured the duke, and his brothers, could expect utter privacy from any lurkers. It meant they would all sleep easier.

Stratford found his own door and slipped inside his chambers. The room he'd always lived in was illuminated by a single candle but was still warm, as the fire had been banked for the night. His bed had been turned down, too, and a nightshirt and robe left out for him to wear. He chuckled to see the evidence of Cuthbert's sense of humor. Stratford had never worn either garment, and only Cuthbert could have told the new man Winston to put them there.

Stratford shrugged out of his coat and waistcoat, untied his cravat, and pulled his shirt up over his head. He rolled his shoulders, aware his muscles, his entire body even, had been tense for hours upon hours. Being around his extended family exhausted him.

He found water had been left in a jug beside the basin and threw some over his face. As he was drying his skin, he happened to see a pair of dainty feet low on the floor of his adjoining dressing room.

His breath caught. There was no reason for any woman to be in his chambers, lest they were bent on seducing him. The only women here were servants or relations. He took a few cautious steps in that direction, gut churning in dread at the inevitable scene that would accompany throwing out a misguided cousin so desperate for marriage that she'd come to him for the role of husband. "Who's there? Come out now!"

All he heard for an answer was a soft snore.

Although that sounded completely harmless, he figured the woman was desperate enough to have waited all this time had fallen asleep. He snatched up a candlestick to take a closer look and crept to the doorway. If they stayed sleeping, he could easily sneak away and perhaps spend the night in the library, thus avoiding any awkward waking and conversation.

Once at the door, he cautiously poked his head inside the space—only to recognize his replacement valet, lying under blankets on the hardwood floor, one foot sticking out toward him. "What the devil?"

Dane Winston did not so much as twitch.

Stratford considered kicking the fellow awake and sending him off to his own room, until he noticed the fellow had his travel trunk beside the makeshift bed, too. It occurred to him that with so many of the family staying at the palace, bedchambers must be scarce. Every guest would have brought servants, and he assumed there were not enough beds to go around. Cuthbert had enjoyed his own little chamber on the floor above and would never have agreed to be displaced. Winston, however, so young and fresh to his service, must not have asserted his authority and kept that room for himself.

A valet of Stratford's should have kept his own chamber, no matter which body was fulfilling that role.

Winston should not be denied the right to use his old valet's bedchamber. He would have to give Winston a severe talking to in the morning about standing up for himself. It wasn't Stratford's place to interfere with the pecking order below stairs, and yet he felt unusually protective toward young Dane Winston.

Stratford raised the candlestick high and studied the sleeping fellow.

Man? Or boy?

By candlelight, he looked even younger...and oddly appealing.

Stratford drew back a little, startled by that errant thought. He liked women, not men. Always. But as he peeked at the sleeping form again, it was hard to believe the valet's claim to be a man of four and twenty years. He peered closely at his jaw. Hardly a hint of beard about him, even at this late hour of the night.

He scratched his own jaw, feeling the scrape of

stubble under his fingertips. By Stratford's estimation, Winston had to be closer to sixteen rather than the four and twenty years he professed to be.

Perhaps, if he were that young, it was better the fellow remained sleeping in Stratford's closet. The other servants could be mean at times to newcomers, and someone so young could be bullied about unfairly. The butler had little to no patience for complaints or unruliness from the servants of Ravenswood Palace, too.

It would not do for anyone to be confused about Winston's gender or inclinations, either.

Stratford decided the lad could remain sleeping in his closet, at least until he got his bearings. He was far too young to defend himself well against larger servants if such measures were ever required.

Winston snored again, and Stratford chuckled softly under his breath as he pulled the door shut. He had employed a tiny hippopotamus to be his valet. It was almost adorable.

Chapter Four

"If you could remain still, my lord," Winston begged as she tried unsuccessfully to put an evening slipper on Lord Stratford's left foot, despite his lack of cooperation for the task. To make herself heard, she slapped her hand to the floor. Hard. "Please."

The foot finally stopped moving long enough for her to attach a shoe to the man, and she heaved a heavy sigh for that small success.

Winston settled back on her heels a moment and looked up sourly. Lord Stratford had been painting since he'd risen that morning, and nothing and no one could seem to divert his attention from his artistic pursuit. Not food, not even being forcibly dressed for an important family gathering.

Six hours standing before the easel, either painting or staring at an empty red dress strewn across his large bed. He was expected downstairs at any moment and was nowhere near ready. She wasn't sure she was paid well enough for the frustration he was causing her today.

Winston was beyond exasperated. Earlier in the day, Lord Stratford had lectured her about asserting herself among the servants, and ensuring she was treated with the respect due her position. But Winston knew too well that respect was earned, not granted immediately. She'd agreed to sleep in the dressing closet to get on the butler's good side from the very beginning. That was absolutely vital.

She had rested well upon that floor, never even hearing Lord Stratford's return. She pursed her lips as she studied the half-dressed lord now. Sitting him down to be shaved had been a nightmare because he kept turning his head to look at his painting and she feared she'd end up cutting his throat. To get the job done properly, she'd had to turn him and the painting to face each other in the end.

"It's no good," he muttered, tossing his paint brush aside with a groan of distress. "No good at all."

Winston stood quickly and risked a peek at the portrait before her current master. If anything, the painting seemed to have lost the glimmer of life it had possessed before he'd started that day. He was painting from memory alone, and it seemed it was failing him badly. "It's not as bad as all that," she lied carefully.

"What would you know of art?"

"Nothing, of course, my lord." Winston knew a great deal about art, but she'd always intended to hide it from him. She had no skill herself. Despite that, Winston had been fascinated by the paintings of her ancestors that had graced her childhood home, and in other places she'd visited over the years. She had studied each one, especially the men in order to copy them. Their arrogance and dignity her best source of inspiration for how to act around others. She hoped for a chance to view the paintings in Ravenswood's long gallery while she was here, too. "It's almost time."

"Yes, time to dance a merry dance with the family yet again," he grumbled, wiping his fingers on a cloth already smeared with color. "I'd rather stay here where its peaceful and paint."

Since the painting was not going well, Winston felt a change of scenery might do Lord Stratford the world of good.

She turned away from him and fetched a clean damp cloth. His fingertips were smeared with fresh paint again despite his rubbing at them, and she fretted he'd wipe them over the white linen shirt she'd already forced him to don. If he ruined that perfectly pressed garment, or the cravat she had painstakingly forced him into earlier, she'd never forgive him.

Winston asked for his hand and carefully began the slow task of wiping the paint from his skin. He had nice hands, hands that were not pampered or as soft as she'd first assumed they would be.

"You have a very gentle touch, Winston," Stratford murmured, staring at the painting still. "Small, like the rest of you."

She turned his hand over with a little more force and rubbed his skin a little harder. "My father was a small man," she murmured. If her father was still alive, he would be much the same, she expected. A little over her height now but older. His grip had been strong, almost crushing to a small hand like hers. Father had constantly complained Winston was not growing fast enough for his liking.

"My own father was on the large side," Stratford confided. "Quite intimidating. I'm the youngest of my brothers and was a constant disappointment to him."

Lord Stratford had not talked of his father much beyond saying he was dead, and Winston was wise enough not to offer a comment on her employer's appealing size. Lord Stratford was lean and well-muscled, but she would not describe him as large, except where it mattered most to men. She kept her eyes firmly on his fingers, but she'd seen him naked enough times to know parts of him were impressive. How could she have avoided noticing when she dressed him each day and he hadn't a modest bone in his body?

She felt his eyes on her as she worked on his other hand and struggled to control a telling blush as she checked for paint under his nails.

"The family is quite used to seeing paint on my fingertips at the dinner table, Winston," he promised in a whisper, leaning in. "Don't worry about it."

"Of course," she agreed, drawing back a little.

But that did not mean she had to accept that near enough was good enough when it came to her employer's presentation. When Winston finally judged his hands clean enough to sit down to dinner with the duke and others, she fetched his gold embroidered waistcoat. He held his arms back so she could slide it onto his shoulders, but he did not assist in tackling the buttons at the front. His entire interest remained on the lifeless portrait on the easel before him.

Winston did not ask his permission to finish dressing him. She simply moved in front of him and slipped each button through their assigned hole, fiddled with the placement of his cravat until it was perfectly arranged, and then looked up.

Lord Stratford was looking at her now with an odd smile playing on his lips. "You know, your eyes are a remarkable color," he murmured. "I can't decide if they are gray or blue."

"I have my father's eyes," she said in as offhand a manner as possible. "As changeable as the weather, I'm told."

"Ah, that explains my difficulty with deciding upon their color," he answered, and his lips turned up at the corners even more. "Yesterday, I thought them almost green when you looked upon Ravenswood," he said, obviously attempting to tease her for wanting something she could never have.

She did not rise to the bait and sought to end

the exchange with her silence, as she had at every turn around him. She did not envy him a home such as Ravenswood, but his fascination and continued taunting was a bad sign. Too much curiosity and Winston risked discovery. She quickly snatched up his coat, the exquisite navy-blue superfine she'd discovered when unpacking, and helped him into it. It was not a garment that required buttoning, so she turned back to gather up his pocket watch and gloves from a table.

She held them out, foolishly admiring him in his finery. He was every inch the lord, and a rich and handsome one to boot. He could have the ladies eating out of the palm of his hand tonight, especially so if they had any idea what he looked like naked the way she did.

Winston withheld a sigh. The perk of this position, and the pain of it, too, was that she had found a man who attracted her and could never do anything about that. It was not a pleasant discovery to have learned about herself. He made her wish for things best left alone. Things other women giggled and whispered about behind their fans.

She had trained herself to be above such desires.

Finally, Lord Stratford began to help prepare for the evening ahead. Adding rings to his long fingers from a crystal tray beside his bed, attaching the heavy gold pocket watch to his waistcoat, and then he slipped several coins into his waistcoat pocket. He strolled to the mirror to admire his reflection, adjusting the collar of his coat unnecessarily. He was utterly perfect just as he was.

"Excellent," he said, smiling slightly.

"Indeed, my lord."

The man met her gaze in the mirror. "I find the my lords grow tedious the longer you are in my employ, Winston. Especially in here. You may call me Stratford or Sweet, if you care to, when we are alone."

She would not dare do that. Formality was essential between them. It helped her remember her place. "Very good, my lord."

His lips quirked. "I'd best be on my way then."

"Yes, I expect so," she said, smiling tightly. Did he ever just waltz out the door without dragging his feet first? "Enjoy your evening with your family."

But instead of turning away, he returned to look at the painting again. His face settled into unhappy lines. "I should never have left Lisette without completing the work, and now I fear it might never be done to my satisfaction."

"I'm sorry."

"Well, it's my own damn fault." He raked a hand through his hair, his frustration palpable.

He took his leave without bothering to explain who Lisette was to him and why the house party no longer seemed enjoyable. He'd been so happy to be coming home yesterday. Even she had started to feel a sense of anticipation the closer the estate had become. Clearly, all was not going well.

With Stratford finally gone down to dinner though, Winston could think of filling her own hollow stomach. She had missed luncheon when she'd been urging Lord Stratford to come away from the portrait and sit down to eat. She tossed the wash water out the window and hung the damp length of cloth used to dry Stratford's face after shaving him, near the fire so it would dry while she was gone downstairs. Then she picked up his largely uneaten luncheon tray, and while she might have considered stealing a bite for herself, she refused to break the rules. She would eat the food she had earned as a servant, with knives and forks and her own glass of milk or whatever would be served to servants, and carried the leftovers out the door with her.

The servants' hall below was a bustle of activity when she arrived, and she quickly handed the unwanted tray to one of the eager kitchen helpers and stepped back against a wall out of the way. The scent of roasted meat in the chamber nearly made her swoon on the spot.

"Dinner for the servants will be later than expected tonight," a fellow servant warned as he stopped in front of her carrying a soup tureen. He tossed his head toward the nearest exit to the garden. "Best wait out in the garden with the others until you're summoned."

Although Winston could have offered to help,

the man was not the fellow to make the offer to. She moved past him and looked for the familiar face of the butler. But she did not see Seymour anywhere. Everyone was rushing about like headless chickens in too small a space. Venturing in farther would only make matters worse. She backed up the way she came and slipped past the kitchen doorway, along a hall that supposedly led to the kitchen garden.

She had been inside all day anyway, and now she gratefully breathed the fresh air deep into her lungs. Winston had always loved the outdoors more than anything in the world. As a child, she'd spent endless hours running about or riding her pony on Father's estate. Fishing, largely without success, or climbing in the highest trees. As a boy, she'd had endless freedom to excel and had been praised for her efforts. As a girl, she would have been called an unruly brat and likely punished for half the things she'd ever done. Even though her life had been a lie even then, she thought of those days with a fond longing time and distance had never displaced.

There seemed to be no one else in the garden, and she strolled along the pathways at her own pace, inhaling the scents of rosemary, thyme, and the summer to come that lingered on the air. What would it be like to run off through the garden gate, wade through the first stream she came to with no care for her clothing or disguise, and then climb a tree at her age? She might wish to stay there until the stars came out.

She might have considered it if she wasn't a valet with a stomach crying out to be filled.

Winston made three more circuits of the garden before deciding to head back to the kitchen doorway. The other servants meant to be out here were obviously elsewhere. Night was deepening and surely the servants would be eating soon.

But when she reached the door she'd used to exit the palace, it was shut tight, although she didn't remember closing it behind her. And although she tried with all her might, it wouldn't open again.

Her eyes widened. Had she been locked outside by mistake?

Winston looked right, beyond the kitchen garden, to the terrace doors open far in the distance where the family must be gathered tonight. She could hear the murmur of many voices, rising over the futile playing of musicians. She could get back in that way but only as a last resort.

Winston knocked and then pounded with her fist upon the heavy, aged wood door until it suddenly flew open. The butler glared out and then scowled to see her standing there. "Servants are expected to attend the dining hall promptly."

"I was told dinner was delayed and to get out of the way until called," she replied angrily.

The butler squinted at her with suspicion. "There was no delay."

"You doubt me?"

"No one employed at Ravenswood would play such a cruel trick," he insisted.

"Well, someone did to me," she insisted, realizing how easy a target she'd been for the mean-spirited lark. Outsiders always were fair game for pranks.

She pushed past Seymour into the palace and headed for the servants' dining room to eat, but saw to her chagrin that only a few of the servants remained there now. Most were rising from the table, fed and replete from the evening meal just served. The servant who'd told her dinner was delayed hid a smirk as he whispered something in Cook's ear that made her laugh as she looked around at Winston.

Winston scowled to be the butt of a joke so soon in her stay. She'd been made a fool of tonight and sent away deliberately so she missed the evening meal and went to bed hungry. All because she was a newcomer. She kept her eyes on the smirking fellow as he carried the last empty plate out the door and into the scullery.

"There'll be nothing now until morning," the butler informed her. "Remember that the next time you decide to take the air."

If confronted about the matter, the servant who'd deliberately misled her would only deny he'd done anything wrong. "I wasn't hungry anyway," she murmured, and stalked away.

Winston returned upstairs to Lord Stratford's chambers, unfed and very angry.

She should have realized there would be greater challenges here than getting her new master away from his work. She would need a better plan for tomorrow, and she'd put some bravado on display when dealing with the other servants.

There was nothing at all to eat upstairs, unless she stole food, which was against the rules. She would have to go hungry till dawn, but it would be the last time she overestimated the kindness of Ravenswood servants. She'd also exact her revenge on the footman who'd misled her before she departed the estate somehow, too. She was very good at spotting the weaknesses of men. They were numerous and varied, after all.

Once in Lord Stratford's chamber, she noticed the dress strewn across the bed. At no time in her life would she ever wear such a delicate creation. She approached a garment that only added to her aggravation. Gingerly, she touched the fabric and rubbed it between her fingers. Soft silk caressed her skin, and she snatched her hand back, unused to the sensation.

The dress could not remain upon the bed. Not when she was in her current bad temper. It must be cleared away or she feared she might take her frustration out on the garment.

Winston snatched up the gown with just two fingers, holding it aloft at the shoulders, and carried it toward the closet as if it would bite her at any moment. But before she could put it away, she caught sight of herself and the gown in the full-length mirror.

She stopped suddenly, squinting at herself. It was almost like looking at a portrait of her mother —albeit without the jewels she'd customarily been adorned with. Winston was so stunned by the resemblance, she pulled the gown toward her body and held it there.

It was like looking at another person entirely. She was not Winston but a lady. A shuddering breath left her lips at the ridiculousness of that thought. If she squinted, she was almost beautiful, as delicate as any other woman she'd ever seen. But that did not please her. A delicate woman she was not, and could never be. She tossed the dress aside in disgust and stared at it where it lay across the hardwood floor.

She was loath to pick it up again.

But she had to because it was her job to keep her master's room tidy. She scooped up the dress just as the door opened.

Lord Stratford strode into the room, nodded to her, and walked into the dressing closet. "Have you seen my opera glasses?"

"No," Winston called, setting the gown aside and rushing to follow him. He began to toss and discard things over his shoulder. Fearing the chaos he was creating, she put a restraining hand on his arm. "If you will allow me, my lord."

Stratford stepped back and let her rummage through the shelves and drawers alone. Winston found the opera glasses wrapped in a wool scarf at the very bottom of a drawer and offered them up to Lord Stratford on the palm of her hand. "There you are."

"Thank you," he murmured, fitting them to his eyes and looking at her through them.

"I hope you enjoy the performance," she murmured, ducking her chin.

"What performance?" he asked as he lowered the opera classes to clean the lenses, then putting them back up to his eyes again.

"I assumed there must be a performance to be viewed if you're in need of those," she muttered, growing uncomfortable with his scrutiny through the magnifying lenses.

"Oh, no. There's no performance to be borne tonight, unless you count watching my family maneuvering for the duke's favor. I was going to do a little spying on my other family members though," he assured her.

Winston frowned. Spying was not the act of a gentleman. "Well, have a good evening anyway."

He laughed suddenly. "Winston, you should see the look on your face. You take every word I say much too seriously. I mean to take a closer look at the portrait of a long-dead relative without having it taken down from the wall. One of the larger ones hanging over the stairs. Something about it has always seemed off to me."

"Oh," she said, understanding. "I thought you meant your living family. The duke's guests."

He laughed and held up the opera glasses again, peering at her through them. "This is how I will survive dealing with them all tonight. I'll study the portraits all over the place, instead of saying something to their faces that would be considered unwise."

She could see his eyes, grown abnormally larger because of the magnifying lens, and struggled not to giggle. He was exaggerating most likely about his family but not about studying the paintings. "Well then."

"Well then."

Lord Stratford nodded and turned away for the door, leaving Winston to pick up the gown again to put it away, smiling to herself because when her employer babbled, he could be amusing.

"I say, Winston," Stratford called out.

Winston turned quickly, holding the gown against her.

Lord Stratford's hand was on the doorknob, but his eyes slowly widened as their gazes met across the room. Winston quickly dropped the gown lower. But Stratford had seen something... and he prowled forward, gaze fixed on her and the red gown she still held loosely in her grip.

Winston's pulse began to pound in her ears the closer he got.

"Lift that dress back up in front of you again," he asked quietly.

Winston could not do that for him. "I was just putting it away until tomorrow," she said, backing farther toward the safety of the dressing closet.

But Lord Stratford was not deterred and continued to advance, all the way to the dressing closet doorway, where he stopped, blocking any chance of escape.

Winston quickly hung the gown on its usual peg. "If you will excuse me."

As she moved to walk past him, he grabbed her arm and held her still. His eyes widened even more when she looked up at him, and he gulped. "Winston?"

He knew. She was discovered. "Yes, my lord?"

His tongue darted out to wet his lips and she couldn't look away as he said, "Have you ever considered wearing a gown before?"

Chapter Five

Winston shook his head, and the disgust at the very idea of dressing as a woman was writ large on his face. But that did not deter Stratford in the least. He needed someone to pose for him that might just pass, if one squinted, for Lisette. The new young wife of a London neighbor was about Winston's height and overall size. Stratford may have been mad to ask such a question of his valet, but they were so similar, he couldn't help himself. Even their hair color was the same. All that was needed was a wig or a bit of imagination on Stratford's part.

It had to be said. Winston could play the role of a female very easily if he were ever to take the stage.

Small bones and a youthful face. Not to mention those remarkably changeable eyes of his. There was something soft in every move he made.

Stratford caught the stunned valet's face between his fingers and gently turned it this way and that, studying the high cheekbones, clenched jaw and pointed chin, wishing the man would smile again.

Winston could pose for him wearing the red dress and a smile while he painted, no one would suspect the end result was an approximation. The valet was exactly what Stratford needed to finish the project without having to trudge all the way back to London just for a few more days of work.

He was needed here more. The cousins were undoubtedly circling the new duke while Stratford was away from the drawing room. Looking at Algernon and plotting how to get their hands on his money, most likely. Not that Ravenswood had any funds to give now, of course.

Stratford's brief study of the ledgers was the final proof of the dire straits the estate was in. He did not doubt Nash's assessment of the situation or the plan to spare their elder brother the embarrassment, either. They all owed Algernon a debt of gratitude for his protection from their father's schemes and wrath over the years.

He wanted to do his part too.

He let his fingers drop away from Winston's face reluctantly, absently noting the smoothness of the valet's skin. How many times a day did the man shave himself to have such smooth and supple skin? He simply could not be four and twenty years with that face. "I will pay you well to pose for me."

Winston drew back, clearly horrified by the idea. "I'm not wearing female clothing for you. I'm no Molly."

"I never imagined you were, and it's not as if I'm asking you to parade about in skirts beyond these four walls." He winced. "That would be embarrassing to us both. I just need you to remain here in the mornings, lying across that bed in the red gown while I paint you."

Winston shook his head. "No."

"Think about it." He drew closer to the fellow. "Tell me what you want by way of compensation and it's yours, I swear."

He could not offer the valet more coin. What he had, or might earn in the near future, was already promised to support the estate for the next few years. But there were riches in his chambers he could share, items far beyond the reach of someone like Winston. The mantel clock alone would be worth the equivalent of five years of his current wages since it was inlaid with gold and ivory. Or perhaps he coveted a permanent position in the duke's household. Stratford could easily recommend him for employment in the family. He was more than satisfied with his meticulous attention to his duties. The new position might not be as a valet, but there were other roles in other households in need of a competent, reliable fellow.

"Should you not return to the duke and his guests?" Winston asked impudently.

"Yes, but..." Stratford flipped the ends of his cravat, which he'd somehow managed to spill a drop of soup on during dinner. He'd intended to take care of that, too, until he'd been distracted by a new source of inspiration for his art.

Winston rushed away to fetch a clean and

pressed replacement cravat and told Stratford to sit in a chair so it could be tied about his neck. Stratford removed his coat and waistcoat to make the job easier for the valet, but he kept his eyes on him as he sat down. The man was turning a deep shade of pink…and doing so as prettily as any woman could in a candlelit chamber.

He put his hands on his thighs and glanced at his current troublesome work. The urge to paint again was strong and nearly irresistible now. "I dread going back down," he murmured, hoping to illicit some sympathy from the valet. He had to find a lure that would convince Winston to go along with his outrageous idea.

He only made a grumbling noise.

"Dealing with my family is a chore," he confided.

The sound came again, and Stratford twisted at the waist, puzzled. The noise had come from the man's belly, not his mouth. He looked up and saw Winston's face becoming an even more alarming shade of pink.

"Are you unwell, sir?" Stratford could not afford to lose the services of a competent valet again. He considered himself damn lucky to have found Winston in the first place.

Winston clamped his hands on Stratford's shoulders and turned him forcefully to face the front again. "I missed dinner."

"How did that happen?"

Winston was silent as he skillfully tied the

cravat back in place from behind, barely touching him. And yet Stratford's neck and scalp tingled as the valet's breath stirred his hair. He gulped, surprised to have that reaction to a man who worked for him. He was hardly aware of Cuthbert whenever he was near.

When it was clear the work of replacing his cravat was done, Stratford turned around on the chair and looked up at his valet's unsmiling face. "I asked you a question, sir. How did you miss dinner?"

Winston sighed. "An accident saw me locked outside."

"An accident?" Stratford could not believe that, given the way Winston would not seem to meet his eyes. "I see."

Had the other servants taken a set against Winston already? New employees were often the butt of jokes and tomfoolery in their first days. He'd known of one London footman who'd been sewn into his bedsheets because he'd snored too loudly. No harm had come of it, other than a harsh rebuke for being tardy starting his duties the next day.

Realizing that Winston might have faced similar treatment annoyed him more than it should. What went on in the servants' hall was really none of his business. But he'd felt a connection to the young man who'd so boldly asked to replace Cuthbert. He'd made Stratford's life infinitely easier so far this week. Stratford could surely do the same for him...and perhaps he'd get what he wanted.

Winton urged him into his waistcoat and left him to do up his own buttons while he fetched Stratford's coat again. "I will eat in the morning," he promised.

"The morning is a long time away," Stratford warned, studying the young fellow. "I also fear your growling stomach might keep me from my rest tonight, or even the entire household perhaps. I cannot have the duke's sleep disturbed for any reason."

Winston snorted a half laugh. "The door between us can be firmly shut. You will sleep comfortably, I swear. So will everyone."

"Well, I'd rather not risk it. You will eat tonight. I will make certain something is sent up to fill that empty belly of yours."

Winston's eyes flew to him, wide and afraid. "Please don't do that. I want no special treatment."

He winked at the fellow. "Leave it to me. They'll never know the truth. I'm already too full of the dinner I just left. Sixteen courses in total. I'll be the size of a barn before we go back to London. Besides, I cannot have you wasting away to nothing. There's hardly any meat on your bones as it is. Whoever comes will say the food is for me, but I expect you to eat it all before I return. "

Winston lowered his eyes and, after a moment, muttered, "Thank you."

Pleased that he was able to do something good

for the fellow, Stratford slapped a hand upon Winston's shoulder. "We can help each other this week."

Beneath his touch, Winston's bones seemed almost as delicate as a woman's. Stratford lifted his hand away quickly, less the moment become too personal and awkward. He couldn't remember touching Cuthbert as if they were equals, or ever wanting to. There were certainly lines that could not be crossed when it came to companionship between master and valet. "I'll be on my way now."

"Yes, my lord."

He smiled tightly, glad that Winston had ignored his earlier offer of informality. Servants did not go around addressing their betters by their given name. He didn't know what had gotten into him to even suggest such a thing. Coming home, and the news he'd learned, had certainly unsettled his view of the world.

He took his leave of Winston before he did anything he might consider foolish and made his way back downstairs. It seemed like the party had largely broken up while he'd been gone but the most persistent cousins still crowded the duke. There seemed to be a heated debate over racing the late duke's inherited thoroughbreds. George Sweet was in the thick of the discussion as usual, urging the duke to run his best during the late summer season.

Crawford was there in the background, but his wife was not.

Stratford sidled up to his friend. "Aren't you glad not to have missed this little get-together?"

"I could strangle your eldest brother for shortening our honeymoon for this if given half a chance," he said with a tight smile. "However, I am grateful for the fuss he's making for my wife's benefit. She's so glad to have his support in front of the family."

"So, tell me, what's it like to have a shackle attached to your leg?"

"By Amity, wonderful." Crawford looked over the gathering. "But the rest of this I could gladly do without."

"At least it was you who ruined her," Stratford murmured, then remembered he should take the opportunity to strike Crawford's upper arm while the incident of Amity's scandal was still largely unspoken of between them. "I should forever be mad had it been anyone else."

"If it's any consolation, she ruined me too. After her, I wanted none other," Crawford promised, wearing a rare blush.

"Yes, I do realize that now too. You were pining away in want of your true love," he teased. He inhaled and let it out slowly. It had been months since Amity was ruined and then disappeared from London, and the shock of her behavior had already largely subsided for him. But Crawford had been acting oddly ever since that night. Moping about, long-faced. Ignoring perfectly good women who would have gladly shared his bed.

Stratford might have suspected something had gone on between the pair if he'd remembered to pay more attention. But at least Amity had found herself a good husband in Crawford, so he couldn't really complain about any of it. Crawford had been his best friend for years, after all. A better man could never be found. "So, you are now a cousin. I don't like very many of those."

Crawford grinned. "I trust I will be one of the few you feel you can rely upon."

"Well, you saved my cousin from her brother's scheming. I suppose I cannot fault you," he said, glancing over his shoulder. Where were the servants tonight? He had a valet to see fed.

Crawford turned to look at him. "So, which is it? Are you mad at me or not?"

"It changes upon the hour," he replied airily and then shrugged the discussion away as he caught sight of a potential problem across the room. "But my opinion is the least of your problems. My loathsome cousin's wife is watching you."

Lady Melody Sweet had once been Crawford's only love. But that was before her marriage to George had separated them forever.

Crawford did not lift his gaze in her direction. "Yes, I know."

Stratford grinned and nodded to the woman

his friend had once loved and lost. Melody Sweet was a vain and jealous creature, even now. Judging by her expression, she was still hoping there was a place somewhere in Crawford's affections for her. "Has she said anything to you?"

"Not a word directly. But she looks daggers at my wife whenever they are in the same room."

Amity and Melody were sisters by marriage. Family affairs like this would forever throw them together. "Best to keep them apart for a while, for Amity's sake."

"That is exactly what the duke suggested I do, too, but I'd already planned to," Crawford promised. "I know which side of the family had my wife's best interests at heart, and those who did nothing to help her."

"You should have known that from the outset," Stratford chided. "Amity is our favorite female cousin, after all." He glanced over his shoulder, worried about how his starving valet was faring upstairs. He hoped Winston understood that everything here took an age to arrange. He hoped the man would also still be awake when he returned to his chambers, to discuss him posing for his painting, too.

Finally, the butler appeared, ordering servants to dispense drinks to each of them. Stratford quickly signaled the man to come closer. "Seymour, I'm feeling a little empty still. Be a sport and have some of tonight's beef sent up to my chambers directly, along with some bread and cheese, too."

"I could bring it to you in the dining room, my lord, if you prefer" he offered.

"No, to my chambers will be better," he insisted. Winston could not possibly come down to eat in the dining room. It would not be proper and would cause him more problems in the servants' hall.

The butler left, and Crawford cast him a troubled look. "What is it with you tonight?"

"What do you mean?"

"You're as nervous as a cat. You keep looking over your shoulder as if you want to be elsewhere. If I didn't know better, I'd say you have a woman waiting in your bed."

Stratford did glance over his shoulder one more time as Melody Sweet slipped from the room.

There was no woman waiting for him, but he was itching to rush upstairs and work on changing Winston's mind about posing. However, he could not tell Crawford about his inspired idea to have his valet stand in for a woman—while wearing a gown. No one could ever know about that arrangement. "Can you blame me for feeling some nervousness to have all the family gathered under the same roof? Every stare feels like a knife in my back."

"That's just a touch dramatic, even for you," Crawford murmured. "Feel free to sit wherever you might feel more protected. There's a spot over there near George, with a good command of the room."

"The most dangerous place in the room is anywhere near a cousin," Stratford complained. "I thought you were my friend."

"Cousin, too," Crawford corrected.

He laughed softly. "I have a painting in the works upstairs that I can go back to if you're going to be that way."

"Ah, another painting has your attention. That explains everything then. You know, I remember the moment you became obsessed with your art. That time, you might recall, it was over that boy you met one summer. You said you wanted to paint him before you forgot the expression on his face, and nothing could stop you painting. Not even the need for sleep."

"I tried." Stratford frowned. "Edwin," he said slowly, recalling the name of an acquaintance. Edwin Aston. A boy Stratford had once tried to befriend, and failed.

It was also the first time in his life he'd had an enemy...besides George, of course. He and Edwin had not gotten along well at all. They had rubbed each other wrong from their very first meeting. Stratford had tried to win Edwin over, but young Aston had rebuffed any and all overtures of friendship. It was funny, actually, that it was the only time in Stratford's life another fellow hadn't wanted the advantage of a friendship with a duke's son.

"It was a very long time ago."

"I bet you still have the painting you did of him," Crawford teased.

"Probably. Somewhere about upstairs, I imagine. I keep them all." All of Stratford's past paintings, failures too, were tucked away in the attics somewhere. Edwin was probably still stored among them. Those paintings were not his best work, but he learned something every time he looked at the old ones.

"Oh, come now!" George Sweet cried out loudly, interrupting Stratford's train of thought. "Surely you're not so miserly that your father's old friends are not welcomed guests at Ravenswood anymore."

"Invitations are at the duke's discretion, not yours," Nash growled, stepping up beside Ravenswood, clearly angry with whatever their cousin had been saying.

Stratford and Crawford exchanged a glance and, by unspoken agreement, moved forward to join the duke as well. "What's going on?"

"George has forgotten his place," the duke noted, eyes flashing dangerously upon their cousin.

"He's invited some of his cronies to the palace without asking if it was convenient or wished for," Nash added in a clipped tone that spoke volumes for his displeasure, too.

"When our grandfather died, your father entertained his old friends for months on end. I assumed you would want to do the same in His Grace's honor," George protested. "I shall tell them all, of course, when they arrive that I have overstepped my bounds and apologize that they must all go away again."

Of course, that could not happen. To turn friends of their father's away at such a time would seem suspicious and rude. Algernon glared. "I shall always honor my father's true friends with the respect they deserve."

George puffed out his chest. "Gentlemen, let us raise our glasses to the late Duke of Ravenswood. May he be looking down at us from heaven with a glass of port in his hand and a smile on his face."

Glasses were raised and the contents drunk.

But Stratford saw a hint of a smile hiding behind George's raised glass. He would wager the invitations had been no mistake. George had planned this chaos well in advance of this moment. He wanted to make things as difficult for Algernon as possible. The added expense couldn't come at a worse time, too. Father's old friends were used to enjoying an excess of amusement when they came to visit.

Unfortunately, many of them were men to whom Algernon now owed a lot of money. Hopefully, George had not invited every single debtor to the palace for the summer festivities.

Stratford stepped forward. "Gentlemen, let us also toast the current Duke of Ravenswood. My brother, and the wisest man still alive. Give him the strength to face the challenges laid down before him, with the cunning of his late father to guide him."

Algernon's lips pressed together as he smiled and accepted the toast as his due, especially when there was a thunderous hear, hear and the stamping of feet from those who surrounded him.

Chapter Six

Winston had expected some form of harassment from Lord Stratford when he'd returned to his room last night. He'd stumbled in seemingly exhausted, stinking of drink, and had gone straight to bed. Not that he should have needed to speak more than a few words to a mere servant, but his low mood bothered her. Her employer was normally an unusually talkative man.

Last night, she'd feared he had discovered her secret when he'd talked about her wearing a gown. But all he saw was a small man who might pass as a woman in a certain light. The relief of knowing her gender was still safely hidden had nearly made her swoon on the spot.

Now that might have been a true disaster. Valets should be made of sterner stuff than a maid.

Winston strode to the window drapes and threw them wide, before putting her hands on her hips to look out at the extensive grounds of the Ravenswood estate. She had seen little more than this view since arriving and the dark kitchen garden when she'd been locked out. Lord Stratford had gone off riding early with his brothers, clutching his head, and she'd been left in peace more or less.

But when he returned, he would likely set to work on his latest and most frustrating painting, as usual.

She glanced over her shoulder at the giggling maids taking their sweet time beginning their duties. They were a silly pair and fond of gossiping about their betters. Given all she'd heard spill from their mouths so far, the house party was going as well as expected.

Drinking and heated discussions were common.

She kept her back to them, not wishing to seem like someone who might encourage a closer friendship, and listened to every word. She wanted to know what issue had pre-occupied her employer last night.

"Did you see the brothers riding out this morning? So very fine."

"I always make it a habit to be near the window facing the stables at seven, just so I can," a maid answered in a whisper, and they giggled again.

"His Grace smiled at me today," one said proudly.

"Just don't be thinking it means anything, Nan. You know he hardly notices whether a servant smiles at him."

"Course he doesn't care about us that way. He's not at all like Lord Jasper. But it still pays to show him kindness. He's grieving for his papa," Nan insisted.

"I'm not sure he should," the other whispered. "His father only got meaner over the years. You heard how he barked when they crossed him."

"I'm glad they're not like him," Nan continued, clearly besotted by the brothers. "None of them are cold…well, except perhaps Lord Nash. I swear when he looks at me, I can't help but shiver."

"He's more pressing matters on his mind, I'm sure, than worrying what we think of him."

"I'd rather him not look at me, Milly. I can still taste that concoction he made me drink when I had a sore throat last winter. Disgusting," Nan said.

Winston shook her head. "At least he didn't suggest a bleeding for a sore throat. It never works."

The pair behind her fell silent.

Winston sighed and kept her eyes on the view.

"Did he mean to talk to us?"

"Who?"

There was silence for a few minutes. "I don't think so."

Winston stood a little taller and set her feet wide apart as she stared out the window, aware she was now being whispered about behind her back. She should not have interrupted the maids' gossiping and drawn attention to herself. But sometimes it was difficult to remain apart from everyone. Hearing the women compare those they served, master and family guests, made her sometimes wish it could be different.

After a few minutes, the pair resumed their prattle in a louder tone.

The duke, of course, was considered the most handsome according to the maids. Ravenswood perpetually wore black, as did a cousin, George Sweet, and it was said to suit the duke better. The next brother, Lord Nash Sweet, might have been as handsome if he might ever attempt a smile. His two sons were somewhere about upstairs in the nursery with a rather stern governess presiding over them. Nan and Milly, the maids, never mentioned a mother for the children, she noted.

The next brother, Lord Jasper, sounded like a devil, having seduced every unrelated female houseguest—including married women—since he'd been old enough to drop his own trousers. They thought his favor worth dying for.

Winston rolled her eyes in disgust. Maids had no good sense. She could not understand throwing away a perfectly good position and reputation for such a dubious thrill herself. There wasn't a man alive she would give her virtue to. Of course, in her current guise, no man would realize she could be seduced, either.

Then there was some talk about Lord Stratford, her employer—a man all the maids swooned over but who never seemed to remember their names. They fell over each other to be helpful still. They thought him the most charming and the friendliest of all the Sweet brothers.

At least they were not so foolish as to imagine any of the family could ever have honorable intentions for any woman who fell for their charms.

"If there's nothing else, sir, we'll be on our way," a maid called out.

Winston turned and surveyed the room. She judged it done to an acceptable standard and waived them out.

The maids curtsied and offered hesitant smiles as they left the room together, which Winston did not dare respond to in kind. They resumed their gossip as soon as the door was closing behind their backs. Once Winston was sure they were gone, she exhaled in relief and then moved to uncover the painting Lord Stratford was currently working on, expecting his return at any moment.

Her employer did not like anyone to view his unfinished works. She could understand why when it came to this particular one. She checked his brushes and paints were exactly where he expected them.

Next, she fetched the dress the model had been wearing for the portrait. The dreaded red dress he wanted her to wear for him. It was a gown for a woman of high society. Someone he knew and admired.

Winston paused near the mirror and held it before herself again. Red seemed to suit her complexion, as far as she could tell. She wasn't versed well enough in feminine fashion to really know. The neckline was modest, but the fabric was sheer enough to see a body through. If she dared to wear the gown for Lord Stratford, he would see her body…and too easily realize that she lacked the usual male appendages and had others that screamed her gender.

That had been how her father had discovered she was not male. She'd been away from the manor with him and had to relieve herself. Father, impatient to reach home by nightfall, had told her to do it right there, standing beside the carriage. She'd disobeyed and rushed for the woods to go behind a tree instead. That had angered him, and Father had followed to chastise his son for foolish modesty. She'd already lowered her trousers to squat as women did and been found out.

The red dress would be her undoing if she ever wore it for Lord Stratford.

And, just like her father, Lord Stratford would want to be rid of her immediately.

The door behind her creaked, and she turned to find a man she'd never seen before slip into the chamber and quietly shut the door behind himself. A stranger clad in black from head to toe. The duke and a cousin of his wore black exclusively, the maids had just said, but which one was this man? And why was he skulking about and rousing her suspicions? He looked a bit like her employer, if she squinted, but she could not think him at all appealing.

Winston put the dress on the bed and stepped forward quickly, so he'd notice he was not alone. "Might I help you?"

The stranger froze, his hand still on the latch, and he looked about for her.

Winston studied him as he studied her for a long moment.

The man was heavy set, taller than Lord Stratford, and had none of his presence. He held himself like a lord but did not quite look the part. Was he one of Lord Stratford's brothers?

His lips twitched in a smile. "Ah, I was looking for Stratford."

"He's not here," she answered without giving him a title at all just in case it was the Duke, or even Lord Jasper wearing black for a change. Since he'd smiled, she was fairly sure it was not Lord Nash Sweet.

"Yes, so I see now."

This fellow had an oily look about him. He struck her as dishonest. "Might I offer my assistance?"

"No. No. That is quite all right. I merely wished to have a word with my cousin."

Relief coursed through her. This was not the Duke of Ravenswood or a brother, but perhaps the cousin who also wore black.

"Very good." She ought to get his name. "I'm more than happy to help if I can, sir?"

"No. I'll find him later," the stranger said, offering up a coin to her with another smile. "I'm sure I will cross his path soon enough."

Against her better judgement, she accepted the vail and with a last look around, the man slipped from the chamber again. Winston held up the copper half farthing between two fingers. Such a coin was not enough to buy her silence.

Perhaps he was miserly by habit. But then she shrugged and pocketed the money. She had been paid for information, not her silence.

Winston was just finished laying out the gown across the bed the way it was supposed to be arranged when Lord Stratford returned, disheveled from his early morning ride, and clearly tired. He tossed his hat in her general direction and threw himself in a chair.

She rushed to fetch his hat before it acquired any lingering dust the maids might have missed when they had swept the room. "I believe a cousin of yours was here, looking for you, my lord," she told him quickly as she straightened up.

Stratford removed his gloves one finger at a time and threw them at her, scowling. "Male or female?"

"Male."

He removed the other glove and threw it at her as well. "What did you tell them?"

"That I did not know where you were, my lord, which was the truth. You did not mention your destination or when you'd be back." She inspected the gloves and set them and the hat aside to be tended to at her leisure. "He did not leave a message for you. He said he would find you later."

"A good reason for staying in here all day. Keep up that habit of not saying where I might be found," he requested before sticking one booted foot out.

Winston hurried to help him remove his riding boots. As she gripped the boot at the ankle, his toes flexed, making the task impossible. "A little help would be appreciated, my lord."

"Sorry, I thought I was helping," he murmured, and she caught a ghost of a smile on his face.

It was a struggle, but she managed to wrench the fine leather from his long leg eventually. The other proved just as difficult. Her employer was still in an off mood and determined to do nothing to help her attend him today. "Might I fetch you a drink to improve your mood, my lord?" she offered.

"Do you have a barrel of ale hiding under your waistcoat?"

She reached into her coat and produced a small silver flask. She held it out to him. "For medicinal purposes."

He took it from her, unstopped the flask and took a tentative sniff of the contents. "What is it?"

"Gin. It'll put hair on your chest." At least that was what her father had claimed when he'd given her that flask to carry so many years ago. The gin was rough, and likely not what the lord was used to consuming. She wondered what his reaction would be to the drink.

He took a tentative sip, shot to his feet, and handed her the flask back on his way to the open window to spit it out. He was grimacing when he turned back. "You drink that poison?"

"Every day," she promised. Winston took a small sip from the flask and tucked it away again in her coat. She relished the burn down her throat, knowing drinking was expected of a man. It helped her blend in and roughened her voice. "Shall I fetch you a sherry to sweeten your mouth, my lord," she teased softly.

That made him laugh, and he sat back down again. "Where did you train, Winston? You're more devious than the usual footmen employed at a coaching inn to have gotten me to drink that rotgut."

"Your first instinct was the right one, my lord," she answered. "As to my training, I gather knowledge as I go along."

"You must have learned very quickly."

"Why do you say that?"

Lord Stratford sat forward. "Well, you're so young-looking. Couldn't be more than sixteen years of age with that smooth face?"

"I'm older than I appear," she muttered, picking up the hat and checking over his gloves. He owned a dozen pair but seemed to favor these for the early mornings so far. She laid them out to dry by the fire.

"How old are you then? And don't lie," Lord Stratford warned. "I know you're not the age you claimed to be when I hired you."

"I'm old enough to be a valet."

"No really, I want to know." He stood and drew closer. "Ever since the day we met, I've been puzzled by you. I never know what to expect."

"I'm no different from every other servant. Looking to advance through hard work and grateful to make something of myself in your employ," she replied in as deferential a way as possible.

He scoffed. "Grateful, you say? Then why not wear the gown and help me finish my work."

"I am grateful for the many benefits of this position, my lord, but that does not mean I will wear a gown just to please you," she answered, flustered. The questioning of her age could not be avoided forever. She did look young with her soft, pale complexion.

She snatched up his hat and applied herself to brushing the felt. If she carried on brushing and ignored him, he should eventually go off in search of better company and conversation. Talk to someone more deserving than a mere servant.

He'd had limited patience for her silences in the past. Besides, there were ample guests below who would enjoy conversing with the handsome fellow. Other women who might wear the dress for him, too.

The thought of him offering another woman the chance to pose for him made her speed up her brushing. She'd see them together. The woman would have to perch herself on that bed, thrusting out her bosom.

The brush was suddenly flying across the room from her clenched hand.

Winston blinked and then rushed to pick it up from the floor. But as she bent over, the back of her neck started to burn, and she glanced over her shoulder, suddenly self-conscious.

For good reason, too.

Lord Stratford was staring at her behind like he'd never seen one before.

He stood slowly, eyes lifting to hers, then his gaze dipped to her rear again, which was still turned in his direction.

Winston spun about to face him, attempting to act as if nothing was unusual in the way he looked at her as she headed back to finish her chores. But his approach never faltered, slow and very deliberate in her direction.

She wet her lips as a chill raced over her skin. Danger was near. She held his gaze. "Is there something else I can get for you, my lord?"

His silence had her heart thumping wildly, and then his eyes dipped lower again. He frowned as his gaze lingered on her chest, and the expression deepened as his stare drifted slowly downward to her hips, where her hands rested.

His eyes widened suddenly. "Small bones. Delicate features. The lightest of touches," he whispered, and his eyes narrowed. "I think I am owed an explanation."

"For what, my lord? The gin?"

He was suddenly right in front of her, looking down from his greater height, and she fairly trembled. His fingers reached out and caught her by the chin. "I was mistaken earlier when I said you could pass for a woman."

Winston's pulse fluttered and she knocked his hand aside. "I don't understand?"

"It was wrong of me to say you could pass as a woman wearing that dress," he whispered. "I should have commended you on your ability to wear a gentleman's clothing so well." He stepped back and inclined his head. "My dear, I believe it is past time for a proper introduction."

Chapter Seven

D amn it to hell, he'd employed a woman to be his valet!

Stratford stared at Dane Winston, waiting to hear the woman's real name tumble from her tightly pressed lips. Those eyes, those small hands, that damn lying tongue. Whoever she really was, she was a fascinating creature, but an utter fraud from the top of her head to the soles of her dainty feet.

He cursed his own blindness. He'd known this woman a week without suspecting her gender was not as professed by her manner of dressing.

Dear God, he'd stripped for bathing and dressing, strutting about naked afterward, without thought for the woman's likely shock or sensibilities. His cheeks warmed a little now at that remembrance.

He'd compromised her.

"Your name?"

"Dane Winston."

"Dane Winston? Hardly?"

Her mouth pursed momentarily. "I assure you it is true." She wet her lips nervously.

He blinked slowly, tracking her tongue, but was not about to be deceived or diverted. He was being lied to still. "It's obvious to me now that those hips belong to a young woman."

Winston's cheeks darkened. Her anger at being found out all too apparent. "That's not true."

The red-faced valet turned away, but Stratford was having none of that. He grabbed her forearm and put her directly in front of him again, noticing she was light but not as fragile under his fingers as he'd anticipated. She resisted him. He sensed a strong body, muscled and sleek, and judging from the obstinate set of her jaw, a strong will, too. "Well, not so fast, whoever you are. You and I have a lot to talk about."

The fellow—the young woman—glared at him. "Take your hands off me or I'll knock your block off."

"You won't strike me, not if you wish to keep this quiet," he warned quickly.

The threat of taking a blow from this woman did not worry him, but the threat of creating a scandal, of becoming engaged to her, was utterly unappealing. He'd not the faintest idea of who she was, or who she was related to.

The initial shock was subsiding a little, and Stratford was not letting this creature out of his sight until he had some answers. "The last thing I want to do is marry some chit foolish enough to think that parading about in breeches is the way to catch herself a husband."

"Why would you think I want to marry someone as blind as you?"

She had a point. He had been blind about a few things lately. First Crawford and now this. "If anyone finds out about you, we would not be given a choice." She attempted to shake him off, but Stratford tightened his grip. "Who. Are. You?"

"Your valet," she insisted, scowling up at him. "Employment is all I want from you, I swear."

Stratford studied her face and reluctantly admired her pluck. He wasn't so much angry anymore as embarrassed. He was also curious about why she would have done this to them. She must have known the risk to her reputation upon taking up a position with a bachelor.

A valet's life, and their duties, was not an easy life, either. But then, neither again was a maid's lot, and they often had the men they worked for pawing at them.

Carefully, he loosened his grip on Win's arm, reluctantly admiring the way she did not shrink away from him or run off screaming. She had pulled off the impossible, it seemed. Parading about as a man couldn't have been easy, but she did it so well. How was he to have known it was all a deception?

She must have had a good reason for her masquerade. He did not recognize her from society. But she had been most insistent that he take her on as his valet and accompany him home. "Why would you want to be a valet? My valet in particular?"

She licked her lips again, and a reaction he

needed to ignore assailed him. It was not a gesture intended to arouse his interest, but it had. Stratford liked women. He'd liked Dane Winston the valet from the start. Even when she wouldn't talk back to him.

Stratford had been brought up to protect women, even from the folly of their own actions.

Unfortunately, this she was remarkably handsome when she had worked herself into a temper. Win was not the vacuous sort who usually sought him out for company in society. No wonder he'd always tried to get a rise out of her. Deep down, he'd known she was different. Winston had struck him as an educated and too serious young man. Someone dependable who ought to learn to laugh at the world. She'd also been someone who'd promised not to cause him any trouble.

But women were always trouble.

It would take time to decide how much trouble this mistake of his might cause in the end. Win was undoubtedly a bluestocking to the tips of her fastidious fingers. Being a woman explained Stratford's confusion about her age. She really could be closer in age to himself.

Win shook her head. "Are you ready to change for luncheon?"

"I'm not going to luncheon," he warned her.

"Of course you are," she said as she stepped around him and hurried to pour water into the wash basin, making ready for Stratford to rinse his face before being shaved.

It was exactly what a valet would normally do for him. Yet seeing this particular woman doing the duties of a valet caused him no end of embarrassment. He should have sensed the difference long before now. Usually, he hardly noticed Cuthbert except when he didn't answer him. But when Win was around, hadn't he gone out of his way to make her notice him? He'd been alert to every sound and move she made, which was different to his normal awareness of other servants.

Stratford attempted to take the jug out of her hands. "Give me that," he insisted.

"No. It is a valet's duty," she protested, holding him off.

Stratford sighed. "We both know you cannot continue as my valet," he protested, succeeding in gaining control over the jug at last. "I can look after myself, you know."

"You could have done it every other day, too, but never bothered. Why start now?" Win countered, one brow raised, even while attempting to claim the jug back.

Stratford lifted the jug high to see if she would jump for it.

She poked him in the ribs instead, and he instinctively lowered his arms to protect his sensitive sides. The jug was snatched back and returned to its usual place.

"You fight dirty," he complained. "How have you managed this ruse for so long? You must have had help."

"Wash for luncheon first and I'll explain everything," she demanded, and for some reason, Stratford did as he was told, and threw some water off his face.

He dried his skin and then glanced down at Winston again.

Win.

He would miss Winston the valet. He'd no regrets about hiring that fellow. But Winston the woman was an entirely different kettle of fish.

"Waistcoat off, shirt next," she demanded, all business.

Stratford paused. "So, if you don't want to marry me, I hope you're not here with plans of seducing my brothers."

Win snorted a laugh. "Is that how you view all women? Each with an eye to luring one of you into a marriage? Such arrogance. I'm sorry to disappoint you, my lord, but I'd rather not be that miserable."

Stratford was profoundly relieved by her words, and yet offended by her remark. He wouldn't make his wife miserable. Not deliberately anyway. But many a family would gladly wed their daughter to the new Duke of Ravenswood, or his relations, if they could. Whether she cared for the match or not, too.

He let his gaze skim down Win's body again.

Slender, boyish, with no hint of a bust that he could see even now. He caught Win by the hand and pulled her into his arms, just to be certain his gut was correct. As his hand skimmed naturally from shoulder to waist, he detected thick wrappings held tight to her upper back. "You bind your bosom flat?"

Win wrenched out of his arms immediately, cheeks turning a bright shade of pink. "You cannot be late for luncheon."

At least she reacted like a woman should when pawed at. He put his hands behind his back and winked at her. "No one will miss me yet."

"I'm certain that is not true. The butler made it very clear that your timely arrival was essential to the smooth running of the household." She lifted up a fresh shirt and held it with two fingers at each side, clearly waiting for him to strip his old one off and don the new one.

"Seymour can be a tiresome old windbag at times, forever chiding Cuthbert for my tardiness too. Pay him no mind." Stratford grinned. How very sweet of her to worry that he was not late for his appointments though.

He slowly peeled off his waistcoat, unbuttoned his shirt front, and then tugged the garment over his head. When he came out, he was pleased to see Win's eyes were fixed on his bare chest. He inhaled, and her lips parted slightly.

At least she had sense enough to react in the

usual way women did when faced with a partially undressed male.

He took two steps in her direction. By rights, he ought not to be pleased by her response, or even tease her. But she had entered his service by deception. Taken complete advantage of his desperation. She'd used him.

She had also taken over from Cuthbert so completely, he hadn't even missed the old fellow. He looked down at Win's serious face now, and that small distraction he'd suffered earlier expanded into a much larger fascination with her response to the sight of him.

He was attracted to Win—but was not certain what to do about that. She was technically in his employ, and he did not dabble with servants. But if he was going to have to marry her, at least he would want her.

Except, Win should never have put them in this position in the first place. She should have been living with her family rather than doing the work of a man.

He grappled with his conscience and unexpected lust a few minutes more before putting it firmly aside to deal with later. Win was right. He really shouldn't be too tardy for today's luncheon with family. He had promised to keep the more ambitious and determined family members out of Algernon's orbit as much as possible. And he also had to keep an eye on Cousin George. The man was up to something.

He donned the shirt and reached for the buttons on his trousers. Win instantly turned away to pick up his fresh breeches. It was damned awkward to suddenly be so worried about giving Win an eyeful when he'd never worried about it before. But then he'd also never suffered an erection in front of a valet. He managed to change from one garment to the other in record time, and he was fairly certain she'd seen nothing she shouldn't this time.

He took the cravat from her, and she started picking up the clothing he'd strewn across the floor. His glance landed on her well-shaped rear again, clearly defined by the trousers she wore so well. He cursed silently under his breath for being so blind. Maybe it wasn't a good idea to desire her, but he liked what he saw a little too much. He'd never been one for voluptuous creatures like the woman he was currently painting. All a man needed was a willing woman with all the right parts.

"I can dress myself, and clean up afterward, too," he promised, intending to spare her the chore.

Win snatched up his dirty trousers and shook them at him. "You need a valet. I will not allow you to make a less than perfect impression for your family. I will be blamed for any lapses in your standard of dress."

He pulled a comb through his hair quickly, lest she think of doing that for him still. "What does it matter what anyone thinks of Winston the valet? He doesn't exist."

"I am him." Win thrust a navy-blue waistcoat at him. "Put this on."

His dressing continued in that vein, Win ordering and Stratford complying, and they both fell silent. Win was clearly a proud woman, even caught out pretending to be a man. Someone keen to do her work well even with the discovery of her gender out in the open between them. As she pressed him into a chair to take over the tying of his cravat, Stratford risked a peek at her face from a closer distance.

She really had fooled him, and there was no reason to suspect she wouldn't have gone on fooling him for considerably longer if he'd not accidentally stared at her well-shaped rear. There was good reason to get rid of her before anyone found out. However, someone as skilled would be impossible to find until Cuthbert returned. And he did need a competent valet. Someone who could keep their mouth shut and attend to the maintenance of his wardrobe. But Win was a distraction he'd no time for at the moment.

When luncheon was over, he would have to sneak her out of the manor and send her on her way. Somewhere more suited to her gender. Somewhere safe from lecherous men like himself. Perhaps she could go off as a companion or even as some poor fellow's wife. He conceded that a woman used to acting a man might not make a comfortable marriage partner. Not unless the fellow was understanding or—he pulled a face— completely as clueless as he'd been.

There wasn't much that was soft about Win at that moment. She was currently scowling at him again. "What are you waiting for, my lord? Go!"

He winced. Definitely a woman to have taken that tone with him. "You'll need to stay here until I get back."

"Will I?"

"Yes. I do need to join my family, but we have much to talk about."

"Do we?"

"Yes, you promised me answers," he reminded her.

"I recall no such promise," she claimed.

And with a sudden burst of clarity, he realized that Win never intended to explain her deception. All her rushing about and getting him ready for the family luncheon had been in preparation for separating them. He scowled back at her. What did she intend to do while he was busy elsewhere? The not knowing bothered him a great deal.

"No one knows about you yet, and I am certainly not about to tell anyone I hired a woman to act as my valet. I would be laughed out of the house."

She did seem a little embarrassed by that. "I wanted this position. If I had realized you were so ridiculous, I never would have let you employ me, either."

"Ridiculous. Well, that's calling the kettle black. It is not me wearing trousers when you should be wearing skirts and spending your days embroidering. But we are stuck together for now. There are worse things in life, surely, than remaining in a luxurious bedchamber for a few hours."

Her gaze flickered about the room, and with a start, he realized she remained as unimpressed by their opulent surroundings as she had been upon seeing the estate. "All I'm saying is, let's talk this over before we do anything that cannot be undone."

She snorted inelegantly, just as any man might.

Stratford went to the mirror. As usual, he looked as well presented as ever with Win's help, but he fussed before the mirror a while longer, keeping an eye on what the valet was doing behind his back. Tidying up but also peeking out at the front drive.

No matter what Stratford had assumed, a sliver of doubt remained. Was he truly certain that Winston was a woman? He glanced down at his groin and thought about peeling Winston out of those clothes, sitting her on his lap and…

Well, his cock thought that an excellent idea.

He groaned.

He glanced at Win again. She needed his protection and his help to keep her secret. The only way he could keep Win safe was to make sure she had no opportunity to stumble right into a disaster. Who knows what might happen then?

They would end up married, that's what.

Win was still fussing with taking his clothes into the dressing closet, uncaring of the oncoming disaster about to befall them both. It was the perfect time to let her slip away on her own, and yet he followed her to the closet doorway instead, worried that she might leave.

She was not fussing with his clothes but was near her makeshift bed, fiddling with something he could not see beneath it. "Winston," he whispered.

She jumped guiltily and did not look up immediately as she answered. "Yes, my lord?"

In the shadows and close confines of the dressing closet, he cursed the risk he was going to take with a bachelorhood he had always been committed to. "Win?"

She looked at him at last. "Yes?"

Stratford reached out, caught her by her upper arm, and drew her to her feet. He caught her chin in his hand, feeling the softness of her skin, the telltale lack of whiskers under his fingertips.

Win was a woman.

There was no escaping the truth.

This remarkable woman played the part of a man well, but now he knew the truth, he could not pretend. A feeling he'd rarely experienced before except around his closest family grew stronger. Protectiveness and a desire to keep her near at any cost.

Before he thought better of it, he leaned down and stole a kiss from her lips for one final confirmation.

Win froze and did not kiss him back. But she did not move or attempt to strike him for his impertinence, either.

Stratford stole another kiss, teasing her lips apart with the gentle and persistent swipe of his tongue until he got a reaction.

A shocked gasp spilled from her lips, and he took complete advantage. He kissed her properly —and became stiff as an iron spike.

He was definitely kissing a woman, and one he liked very much.

He sealed their lips together and held her close, allowing desire to overset good sense.

As her hands landed on his chest, he fully expected to be shoved away. But Winston seemed uncertain of what to do or how to stop him kissing her. He, however, had no such trouble knowing what to do. He cradled her head between his hands and softened his kisses until their lips were inches away. "You're definitely a woman I want to know everything about," he whispered.

But there was no time for any further discussion or indulgence. He was late, and he had to ensure Win remained until he could return to continue with his pleasant interrogation.

He released her and stepped back. Win swayed

there, a look of utter bewilderment on her face. Stratford didn't dare relish the stunned expression for too long. He turned on his heel, strode away to rummage in a desk drawer, and palmed a key before turning back to her, determined to do no more wrong.

Then he left, locking her inside his chambers so she couldn't run away while he was elsewhere.

Chapter Eight

Winston paced and raged in silence as evening slowly fell over Ravenswood palace, her leather shoes making little noise upon the luxurious carpeted rugs. She'd been locked inside Lord Stratford's chambers all afternoon, with nothing to eat or drink but gin from her own silver flask. The manipulative bastard had kissed her, smiled about it, and then locked the door to his bedchamber as he'd waltzed out the door, halting her plan to make a discreet and speedy exit from the estate before he came back.

It unnerved her that he was so calm after discovering her true gender. The kiss had seemed unplanned but was so brazenly done, she could still feel the effects of the first kiss of her life even now. She wanted to loathe him for it, and yet…it hadn't been unpleasant. Until now, she'd always held herself apart from the base impulses of her gender and the men she tried to emulate, and had disdained the gullible women who fell for their lures and false flattery.

Did that make her one of the weaker sex now?

She put her hand to her empty belly. She was growing anxious about what was keeping Lord Stratford away. He threatened marriage. She hoped he wasn't serious about that. Although if he was…

She sank into a chair, mortified.

At least he knows how to kiss.

She raked a hand through her short hair and growled under her breath. Lord Stratford had not come back to change for dinner yet and the realization that the day was nearly gone made her doubly cross with him. She did not want to leave the estate in darkness. There could be thieves hiding in the woods who would waylay any unwary traveler and take what little she would have.

She sat back in the window seat again and put her hands flat on her knees, attempting to find some semblance of calm. She should never have taken on the position as valet to the lord. Handsome, charming men were turning out to be more trouble than she cared for.

She should have let Lord Stratford tie his own cravat. But the next time she got her hands about his neck, she'd most likely want to strangle him with the freshly pressed linen.

She glanced at the clock on the mantel and noted the time was crawling by. The evening meal would be served soon, and Sweet family dinners tended to go on for hours and hours. The servants would certainly have noticed by now that she'd shirked helping but were likely too busy to come find out what delayed her. They would chide her for laziness when they did. If they did get that door open, they'd soon realize it wasn't her damn fault but her scoundrel of an employer.

She fiddled with the window latch and opened the window to look down. Below her was an unappealing long drop to a flagstone path. There was nothing to cling to if she attempted to climb down either.

She closed the window and sat back facing the door. When it opened, she'd be ready to sprint to make an escape.

Unfortunately, when it burst open at last, it was slammed and locked promptly again behind Lord Stratford. He looked about the room quickly, even as he slipped the key into his shirt front. "I had a bet with myself that there wouldn't be anything broken as a result of a feminine fit of temper."

She bared her teeth at him. "Your head may be in danger the minute you get any closer."

He merely laughed at her threat. "I'm pleased to see you also did not attempt to climb out the window. Believe me, the drop would bring a lingering death. I bring a peace offering," he said, gesturing to a sack she hadn't noticed.

She eyed the lumpy sack sourly, heard the clank of glass inside, but was unwilling to be diverted by its contents. Lord Stratford didn't heed her lack of curiosity. He proceeded to lay out a feast upon the very bed he wisely put between them. Bread, ham, cheese, fruit, and even a bottle of wine and glasses. He gestured her toward it all as if she should be pleased.

Her stomach growled but she held her ground. It had been hours since her last meal, but she could wait until she was free.

"Come closer. You must be hungry again," he begged, producing a knife to cut the cheese with. "I won't bite."

"I am not afraid of you," she assured him, remaining where she was. She was a little afraid, mostly of how relieved she was to see him and that he'd returned alone.

He patted the bed again. "Come and eat with me then since you are so brave."

She shuffled her feet, unwilling to be lulled into trusting him. "Are you not expected to join your family tonight?"

"I've cried off. Told my brothers to bear the chore of dealing with our cousins without me for one night."

"Were they happy about that?"

"Not truly, but I was so helpful today they did not complain very much."

Curiosity got the better of her. She'd spent the whole of her day alone or with him. What went on out there seemed a world away. "What did you do today that was so important?"

"Oh, the usual brotherly duties. Deflected the attention of any unsuitable woman trying to catch my esteemed elder brother alone. You have no idea how often the silly twits have tried to catch his eye with the hope of eventually marrying him."

She relaxed a little. "Does he not want to marry?"

Stratford grimaced. "He must, of course. But none gathered here have the size dowry a duke requires to make a match with them. They are all cousins. The duke will go to London for a bride in due time."

Winston understood the responsibilities of a firstborn son only too well. She'd been lectured on the subject numerous times. Increasing the wealth and importance of the family was closely followed by the need to marry well and get an heir and a spare when she was the right age. That had been Mother's problem. She'd possessed a large enough dowry and connections to catch herself an important husband but had only delivered a solitary daughter after a string of failures in the years before. To this day, Winston had no idea how the woman had intended to dupe anyone into marrying Winston. "The money issue."

He looked at her strangely. "What do you know about that?"

She shrugged. "There's never enough, is there? Not for important families like yours."

Lord Stratford exhaled and then patted the other side of the bed one more time. "I really must apologize for being away for so long. I had not intended to keep you locked in all afternoon. But I couldn't trust that you would remain when my back was turned. You had the look of someone planning to run away from me."

"I imagine that happens often," she bit out tartly.

"Less often than you might think," he promised with an instant smile. "You were ready to do anything for me even back at that inn, remember," he reminded her.

She shrugged, refusing to rise to the bait of defending her decisions. She'd be gone as soon as he let down his guard and he would never see her again. It was clear she could no longer work for him, and she certainly would not stay to marry him.

Winston approached the bed slowly to pick up an apricot. She bit into it and nearly swooned from the taste. It had been a long time. She'd not the money to waste on expensive indulgences like this. The fruit was ripe and full of deliciousness, and she wiped the back of her hand across her mouth to catch the drips.

Stratford chuckled softly. "You ape the ways of men very convincingly. My brother did that very same thing at luncheon today. You should have seen the aunts scowl at him for such a display of bad manners at the table."

Was there any point in denying the truth. "I've had a long time to practice."

Stratford gobbled up a slice of ham and then nodded. "Tell me about that."

"Not much to tell. A man gets along much better with the world than a woman."

"Ah, yes, I suppose that is true."

Winston picked up the knife to slice some cheese and put it down close to herself. If Stratford got too close again, she was not unwilling to defend her virtue. She ate well and then got up from the bed, keeping hold of the knife. "If you'll excuse me, I am expected downstairs in the servants' hall."

"No," Stratford replied immediately. "I am not about to be distracted by your sterling work ethic."

She swiveled to stare at him. "I beg your pardon."

Stratford had also risen up onto his knees. "You are not leaving this chamber tonight."

She raised the knife. "You cannot hold me prisoner."

"There's no need to fear my intentions, Win."

"I'm not afraid of you."

"I can see that. But it has not escaped my notice that you are rather unique. You're an extremely competent valet, for one. But you are also a dressed as a young fellow, disguising a woman's body. That could draw the wrong type of attention out there. There are men who like the look of handsome young men, too. And you are alone in the world when you do not have to be."

"I've done all right protecting myself so far," she promised.

He raised one brow. "Have you?"

She squirmed. "There might have been a few situations that could have turned dangerous. But I am nimble and quick to make the right choices."

"I have given the matter a great deal of thought during the time we were apart and have come to one conclusion. You must stay." Stratford gestured to the room. "This is an extremely large house and full of servants and guests. There is no reason anyone should suspect you if you continue to act as you have been and avoid striking up friendships with other servants."

"That isn't a problem for me," she promised.

"As much as it goes against the grain, you will continue in your role as my valet until the guests have gone on their merry way. And then we will discuss what happens next."

"Cuthbert comes to resume his duties, and I leave, of course," she reminded him.

"If that is your wish by then, so be it." He grinned suddenly and sat down again. "There could always be a position for you among the maids here."

Winston wrinkled her nose. "Are you suggesting I wear a dress again?"

"Have you ever worn one...or been kissed before, for that matter?" He laughed as her face warmed with the heat of a blush. "I'm merely pointing out an alternative you might not have considered. I assume you have all the usual feminine attributes hidden under those clothes."

She scowled at the way he was regarding her, trying to see if she had breasts no doubt. He had a decidedly wolfish look about him now as his gaze traveled across her chest and then dipped lower. It was an expression she was instantly distrustful of. "You'll never find out."

"A pity. I quite enjoyed kissing you." Stratford pursed his lips and picked up the bottle of wine. He uncorked it and poured two glasses. "Now this is a far better drop for a gentleman than that poison you offered me from that little flask of yours."

She held his gaze a long time. Despite all the warnings in her head, she had enjoyed Stratford kissing her. However, she would not dare tell him that. "Are you going to be trouble for me?"

"Of course not. I would never force a woman into my bed. I don't have to." He smirked again and held out a glass of wine to her. "Let us toast to our arrangement."

"What arrangement?"

"To cause no trouble for each other," he suggested. "The last thing I want is a scandal or to be married."

"I feel the same." She could drink to that. And did. Downing the glass in one unladylike long gulp. Stratford chuckled but said nothing about her mannish behavior. She backed away from him. "Excuse me, my lord."

Lord Stratford rolled onto his stomach to

watch her go, kicking up his heels up behind him. "Where are you going now?"

"To sleep, of course, since you can obviously have no further need of me tonight."

"But the bottle is not empty, Winston. There's an unbreakable rule among men that once opened a bottle must be consumed until the last drop."

She regarded him with suspicion. She'd never heard of such a rule and yet many men did drink until there was no more in the bottle. Many fell asleep where they sat, too. And if Stratford did that, she could retrieve the key from down his shirt and be ready to leave at first light.

Winston was not expecting to sleep when she went to bed tonight.

"Cuthbert would not have hesitated to finish these two bottles with me, but then again, he is rather better at his job," Lord Stratford murmured, turning away from her. "An excellent man and companion, too. That is why the best valets command the highest wages."

She squinted at the back of his dark head, suddenly realizing she was clearly not being paid the same as Cuthbert. But she was doing everything just as well. "How high?"

"Stay and I might tell you."

She returned to the other side of the bed to look at Lord Stratford's face. He had his nose in his glass, so it was impossible to know if he was in earnest or merely teasing her again.

"If this is some trick to bed me—" she began.

"I'd sooner drink alone, Win," he promised, swinging the glass wide. "Your virtue is quite safe from me. Besides, lovemaking should be fun. At least it is the way I do it."

"Is there more than one way?"

"Indeed, yes." He suddenly laughed, pointing at her face. "Dear God, you must be a virgin to be blushing so hard. My, my. Not male and not even bedded yet. What a shockingly dull life you must have had before coming into my employ."

"It's been more trying than anything else since," she taunted, fighting down her blush. He was the most frustrating man she'd ever met. His strutting about naked had been startling…though not entirely unpleasant.

She caught sight of a ghost of a smile hovering on his lips and then he brought the glass back to his mouth. He took a sip and sighed. "An excellent vintage. I'm glad I picked these two bottles from my late father's private stock, especially to sweeten your heart toward me after locking you in all day. A pity you have no appreciation of fine wines."

"It was tasty," she assured him. Wine was much like everything else. Consumed and forgotten.

Lord Stratford's lips turned down in clear disappointment over her words. He seemed to feel things different than most men she'd known.

She helped herself to another glass.

"Try sipping it this time instead of gulping it

down," Stratford suggested. "Hold the flavors in your mouth a moment."

She tried it his way, and then swallowed.

"Better?"

"Not worse," she replied quickly.

He laughed. "That is what I like about you, Winston. You're very hard to impress."

She didn't think she was that particular, but it never helped to show partiality to something she might miss one day. Like him.

She shook her head, unsure where that thought had come from. She could not like her employer too much. It wouldn't be proper for a valet, or for her, either.

He patted the bed beside him, suggesting without words that she should join him again. And she did.

"Now let me tell you the story of this vintage. It was stored way at the back of the late duke's private wine cellar, never to be touched. An area we were never allowed near while he was alive, I must add. Now that he's gone, there is nothing beyond our reach." He jerked his thumb toward the door. "My brother isn't as much of a curmudgeon as our father was. In fact, and tell no one this, he's my favorite brother. Practically raised me. You'd never know the kindness of his heart just by looking at him."

"I'm glad. You have other brothers, too?"

"Yes, my other two brothers are a different matter altogether. I'm excessively fond of Jasper, he's a bare year older than me, but should never be trusted around women who wish to keep their virtue," he looked at her pointedly, "and my second-eldest brother, Nash, well…if he ever smiled, our society might never be the same again."

"He is unhappy being second born?"

"I hardly think so. He worries to excess over everything, especially over Ravenswood's health," Lord Stratford confided. "The veritable old woman among us. Fuss, fuss, fuss."

"I heard the maids talking earlier," she said, studying the color of the wine. It was prettier in crystal than pewter. "They said Lord Nash is married and has children."

Lord Stratford drained his glass. "Yes. He never sees them. Acts much like my father did with us."

"Is his wife here? I've not heard her mentioned."

"No, she isn't here anymore," he said, and it was clear it was not a topic he wished to discuss with her.

"Sometimes that is the way it should be," she answered, thinking of how tense her family had been. Her own Sunday presentations to her father, before attending church with Mama standing between them, had been awkward affairs and necessarily brief. Winston had been in awe of her father as a child. She'd wanted to please him even to the point of wishing she had been born male all along.

She glanced at her employer, fearful he'd heard the wistful tone in her words, but he was staring into his cup, thinking she assumed. She picked up the second bottle and studied it a moment before setting her teeth to the cork and pulling it free. She poured a glass and topped up his.

Lord Stratford held the glass up between them. "I really do think this is the finest vintage of any I've drunk here at the palace, and believe me this is not the first night I've shared a glass or four with my valet."

"Of course."

"Do not turn agreeable on me now, Winston. You've turned my view of the world upside down and it's not quite settled yet." He gulped down his wine and then looked at her sideways before he waved his empty glass in her direction, ready for another top up.

Winston carefully filled it to the brim, deciding to get her employer good and drunk tonight so he might fall asleep sooner than later. "There you go, my lord."

Her employer drew in a deep breath over the glass, inhaling the scent of the wine, and then sighed. "Win."

"Yes, my lord?"

"Do you think you'll ever marry?"

She tensed. "Why would you ask me that?"

He put one arm behind his head and wriggled

into a seemingly more comfortable position, without spilling a drop of wine from his glass. "Cuthbert thought he might like to be a husband one day. My elder brother must marry, of course. My second-elder brother did marry, but didn't care for it." He shook his head. "Jasper swears there's no reason for either one of us to ever take a bride. Now, with you masquerading as a fellow bachelor, I do wonder at your opinion, too. Surely you want something more than servitude all your days."

"I expect not to marry," she said slowly.

"Hmm, do you not find men at all attractive?"

Warmth crept up her cheeks and she struggled with how to answer him. She found him pleasant to look upon, especially naked, and was enjoying their conversation tonight, now he knew her secret. But marrying a man, any man, had never truly crossed her mind. To marry a woman, and keep up her charade, would be pointless. It could never be more than chaste companionship she shared with any bride.

To marry a man, however, would mean she'd have to change herself completely to please him. Wear dresses, mind her manners, become all the things she despised so much about her mother.

She was better off as she was. Living life on her own terms; keep moving about the countryside to new places of employment. Desire, attraction of the kind Lord Stratford wondered about, played no part in her plans.

She turned to tell him so, but he let out a loud snore.

Winston hurried to reach over and carefully took the glass slowly falling from his fingers without waking him, saving the bedding from a spill of red wine. She sat back, regarding the two glasses she held, and then drained both before considering the half-drunk bottle. It was a shame to waste the bottle, and there was that rule.

Winston shrugged and refilled her glass.

"Excellent vintage," she told the sleeping young lord as she took a dainty sip.

In sleep, Lord Stratford seemed so carefree and attractive. He had a nice face…straight brows and thin, strong lips. Lips that had touched hers and set her senses on fire—at least for a moment today. She blushed again at the memory.

But kissing her again tonight had clearly been the last thing on his mind and the last thing she should ever want him to do. He'd only kissed her earlier to rattle her, and perhaps to confirm his suspicions that she was in fact a woman.

She finished the wine and hugged her knees, watching him sleep so peacefully beside her.

Despite everything, she would like to stay in Lord Stratford's employ, talk to him again like they had spoken tonight. A little teasing. A little fun and flirtatiousness between them now and then, perhaps, as well. It would amount to nothing, of course, but she'd never had that with anyone before. She had quite enjoyed their sparring. Winston had never had a real friend. She'd always needed to keep other boys at arm's length.

Again, that feeling of Stratford being familiar returned. She couldn't recall ever seeing him upon the long road of her wandering life. Perhaps she'd known him before that time.

Winston went cold all over at that thought. She sincerely hoped she had not known Stratford before her father had taken steps to be rid of the embarrassment of her existence.

Chapter Nine

Stratford paused to look behind him. "Winston, do hurry up or I'll miss the sunrise!"

Lower down the slope, he heard a few unkind utterances shouted back from his struggling valet's saucy mouth. He smiled and drew in a deep breath of fresh morning air.

Stratford had awoken that morning with the unstoppable urge to be in the outdoors painting, so of course, he needed to take his valet with him to carry his easel and paints. It was either that or spend the day wondering if Win might have been found out or fled while he was gone.

It was good to be out of the palace for a while, too. There was only so much of his extended family he could take. And none of them had mentioned plans to leave the house party early, much to his disappointment.

He glanced over his shoulder to watch Win continue to struggle up the hill. Stratford had truly underestimated the depths of her stubbornness. He'd offered to help carry the easel some time ago and had been roundly rebuffed. But now they were far beyond view of the palace and there was little need to keep up appearances.

He charged back down the hill. "Give me that, woman."

"Do not call me that," Win hissed, trying to avoid his outstretched hands.

"Why not say it here? No one could possibly hear me. If I did it in the palace, you'd have the right to complain," he promised and reached for her waist as she stumbled. He caught her easily and righted her again. "For heaven's sake, the easel is twice your height. Give it to me before one or both of you become broken," he demanded, and succeeded in taking the easel and everything else from the woman pretending to be a man still.

"Damn it," she complained, staggering the rest of the way to the top before collapsing on the ground untidily. "I should have been able to manage. I'm sure Cuthbert would have," she said in a tone that mimicked a woman complaining about a comparison he hadn't even made.

"Cuthbert would have made two trips," he assured her.

She gaped, causing Stratford to laugh at the stunned look on her face.

Now that he knew Win was merely aping the ways of a man, and a valet, too, he couldn't help but find everything she did this morning highly amusing. "Tell me, how long have you gone about pretending to be a man? Surely I'm not the only one to be fooled."

"Long enough."

"No, really, I must know."

She shrugged. "All my life."

"All?"

"Indeed."

"My word! Even from the cradle? That is remarkable. No wonder you used your teeth to pull the cork from that second bottle we drank last night." He put his hand to his head. "At least my aching head is almost gone. How is yours now?"

"My head wasn't aching to begin with," she assured him.

He shook his head and looked at her again. "Even more remarkable. I suppose next you'll claim you could drink me under a table anytime you want."

"It wasn't me sleeping on the floor next to the bed this morning," Win reminded him. "I can handle my liquor far better than you, apparently."

"Sleeping on the floor was a conscious choice on my part," Stratford promised with a shrug. "I did not want to wake beside you. You've already threatened my life should I fail to resist your appeal."

"You should have woken me, and made me sleep on the floor rather than your bed," she complained, scowling fiercely. "I'm sure Cuthbert never would have been allowed that dubious honor."

"Indeed, no. However, you had climbed under my blankets by that point, complaining that I let you forget about the fire enough that it died out, if I remember correctly. I couldn't see the harm in letting you enjoy a little comfort. It didn't hurt you to sleep in a proper soft bed. But I admit, I did briefly consider carrying you to yours. However, I came to my senses quite quickly. I feared you might get the wrong idea about what I was trying to do and attempt to inflict real harm on my person," he promised, discretely covering his groin.

The sight of Winston curled up on his bed had been one of those defining moments of self-discovery and ruthless restraint. He had wanted to stay with her in bed. Pull her into his arms and hold her while she slumbered. Yet until she thawed toward him, he wouldn't dare assume they shared similar yearnings for each other. He would treat her as the valet she insisted upon being to him.

He placed a picnic blanket beside her. "Spread that about."

"Yes, my lord."

Stratford moved the easel to one side of the blanket and then sat himself down right in the middle. "You can sit at my feet, Win," he said, holding back a grin at how much fun he seemed to be having, saying things that clearly set her teeth on edge.

"How very generous of you, my lord," she ground out, but did sit herself down on the very edge of the material.

Because she was in front of him and offering a splendid view of her rather elegant rump,

Stratford had trouble dragging his gaze to the sunrise that had brought them both from the palace so early in the day.

But he succeeded just as the sun peeked over the horizon. He held his breath, as he always did at such moments, and watched the colors of the sky change. Eventually he looked away and saw Winston staring out over the waking valley below them with a wistful look on her face. In the morning light, knowing what he knew now, Stratford was struck by how familiar Winston and this moment seemed to be.

Winston was a stranger to him, and yet the more time they spent together, the more he was sure they had met somewhere before. Long ago. He shook his head because that would mean he'd been a fool twice with her.

Winston suddenly turned. "Can I ask you something that might seem impertinent?"

"Yes, anything at all, Win."

"Do you trust all the members of your family?"

"That is impertinent, but I'll answer it anyway." He sat forward, smiling at the woman. "I trust my brothers, and of course my cousin, Mrs. Amity Crawford, and her husband are good people. Uncle Henry isn't so bad in small doses."

She nodded. "That fellow who came to your chambers yesterday. The one I told you was looking for you."

"What about him?"

"I…I didn't trust him."

"Who did you say it was?"

"He did not give his name. He wore black."

"My brother the duke wears black out of respect for our late father, as does a cousin."

"If you'll forgive me for saying this, he had an oily look about him."

"Ah, that would be Cousin George you met most likely instead. Your instincts were correct about him indeed. A man not to be trusted."

"He gave me this. I suppose it was to buy my silence about his visit to your room," she said, revealing a copper coin.

"Well, he's certainly the tight fist of the family when it comes to trying to buy information."

Win tucked the coin away. "I was better tipped at the inn."

"Ha. By me as well, too," he crowed.

She sighed and drew her knees up tight to her body and looked out over the valley again. "Yes, if you had stayed much longer, you'd have come home with pockets to let. There's no reason to pay everyone so handsomely."

"I value good service," he promised. "Your last employer is a good man."

"The innkeeper saw you coming," she warned. "Told us all to be especially nice to you because you tipped so excessively. He has a number of unflattering views of higher society that I'm sure you don't know about."

"Is that so?" he rubbed his jaw. The innkeeper

had been especially happy to house Cuthbert during his recovery. Promising to send the bill later. Now he was worried about the debt he might incur. Stratford had thought the innkeeper a fine fellow but what if he'd been deceived there, too? "I shall never be as tightfisted as Cousin George but will consider pinching a penny or two next time I visit that particular inn. You'll have to tell me how he takes it."

She shook her head. "I won't be there the next time you stop."

"Why wouldn't you go back?"

"It was time to move on," she said solemnly. "I never allow myself to get comfortable anywhere."

"Oh," he said, feeling disappointed that he might not see Winston again. He hadn't fully considered what keeping a secret like hers might mean. She would always be at risk of being found out. It couldn't be an easy way to live. "Where will you go?"

"I don't know yet. I never do. I just set out and see what opportunities await."

"Why not go home?"

She sucked in a breath. "I can never go back."

"I suppose your family doesn't approve of you wearing the clothing of a gentleman."

"No, they certainly do not."

"Well, I don't mind. Not really," he promised. He should be at the easel already, eagerly attempting to catch the wonder of the morning in his art. He'd come out here to work, after all. Although spending the morning lazing about in the sun, talking to Win, held a far greater appeal. He scooted down to sit on the edge of the blanket next to her. "Where is home?"

"A long way away," she said unhelpfully.

"Do you miss it? Miss your family?"

"Sometimes. But I doubt I am missed in return. If they saw me again, they'd never claim to know me."

Her words brought him a greater understanding of her retiring nature. She'd been hurt and abandoned by her family. "Well, I would. I would miss you," he said swiftly.

Winston laughed and hugged her knees tighter. "You'll have Cuthbert back soon enough."

"Yes. A valet I would never want to kiss as much as I do you right now," he suggested, wishing she would relax and laugh again.

She turned to look at him eventually. "No, you're not quite the scoundrel you want me to believe, my lord."

"Well, I could be with you, but I've made a rule never to seduce my servants, especially not my valets."

She set her chin on her shoulder. "You said I couldn't be a valet anymore."

"I don't want to dismiss you, but it does make things more complicated—me wishing to kiss you every time you curse me. And you cursed me a lot this morning."

"I don't mean to be rude. It's just… This is so strange. I'm not like other women."

"You are to me, and that is all the opinion you should ever really care about."

She laughed softly. "Do you always talk nonsense?"

"Not always but often," he promised with a sincere smile. He couldn't help wanting to draw her out because he liked her better than even his last lover. Winston had a way of making him comfortable without trying too hard to win him over.

"I like listening to you," she said—and then suddenly leaned toward him, and her lips landed awkwardly on his.

Stratford was startled but only for a moment. He immediately drew her down to the blanket so he could kiss her properly, show her how it was meant to done. He wrapped her tightly into his embrace, craving the closeness of her body against his. Winston was curved in all the right places except for her bound breasts. He suddenly hated those bindings under his hands. They were coming between them and mutual pleasure.

Knowing he couldn't do anything about them, he moved his hand down her back and grasped her sweet little derriere. The same orbs that had opened his eyes about her gender. He might just love them already.

Winston's arms twined around his neck

hesitantly, and he broke the kiss to stare down at her. "How did I ever mistake you for a man?"

"You saw what I wanted you to see," she assured him proudly.

She was lovely and sweet and fierce. Despite everything, she had earned his respect. He brushed his fingers lightly over her blushing cheek. "Are you a virgin, Win?"

"Yes," she admitted, her blush deepening to a dark pink.

"You'll stay that way, too, with me," he promised before claiming her lips again in a searing kiss that left them both gasping when they parted again. He wouldn't be fathering any brats on Win. That would truly ruin her disguise and ensure they ended up married to each other.

But he'd make love to her. Show her what it felt like to be craved by a man that was wild for her kisses. Someone a man thought desirable no matter the disguise she wore. He was already as hard as a rock in response to her kisses.

He cradled her head, teased his fingers into her short locks and lost himself to passion. It was easier than he'd imagined to make love to a woman who dressed like a man. But it was also frustrating. It wasn't a simple matter to find bare skin to stroke. Every inch but her hands and face was covered in men's attire. However, it was simple to slip his hand from sweet derriere to cup her even sweeter sex.

He pushed between her legs and held her sex

in the palm of his hand. Win nearly jumped out of his arms for his presumption. He grinned cheekily when she scowled at him, "Definitely a woman's body down there too."

He kissed her again and moved his hand in slow circles, pressing palm and fingers over the area until she broke the kiss to gasp out loud. Passion blazed from her eyes. Blue today, the color of the sky above them. When he found just the right spot, she uttered a tiny whimper and her eyes fluttered shut. He kept up the steady pressure, studying her reactions to his lovemaking. Would she allow him to see the moment through to the very end? Did she even know there was one?

He certainly hoped so.

He slipped from her arms and wriggled off the blanket almost entirely.

Winston wore the same style of breaches as himself. Buttons on the fall and then beneath, her virgin sex waited for its first tender exploration. His hands were shaking as he undid one button and then the other on her fall, and he looked up her body to find her watching him.

Her chest rose and fell rapidly, her lips were parted, and her eyes were wide with anticipation.

"Let me love you with my mouth," he begged, biting his lip to await her permission.

Her head fell back and collapsed onto the blanket. "Oh, go ahead."

"Do you not want me to?"

She lifted her head to look at him again. "I don't know what I want or what I'm doing anymore with you."

"Poor darling," he whispered, feeling a touch of guilt for the shocks she must be suffering today in his arms. Passion could be overwhelming even when you know what to expect.

He slowly lowered the fall of her breeches and started to tug upon her shirt to get it out of the way. With the sun warming his back and the woman splayed before him, he grew far warmer than comfortable. He struggled out of his coat and handed it to her to use as a pillow. Then he returned to unveiling the woman he wanted more than anything.

A thatch of pale curls greeted him. He glanced up at Winston in surprise.

"Yes, the hair on my head is dyed brown," she whispered.

"You're a natural blonde?"

"Yes."

"Well, I'll be. Is there anything about you that's honest?"

"I enjoyed the wine last night more than I let on," she whispered. "And talking to you."

"Well, so you should have," he agreed, and then took his bottom lip between his teeth as he eased her breaches past her snow-white hips. He wouldn't remove them entirely, but he required a little wiggle room under the garments.

He lowered his face into her open breeches

and dropped a chaste kiss on her pale curls, and then began to explore in earnest, reveling in her shocked gasps. He tasted a hint of wetness between her legs and lapped, seeking more. A strangled moan left Win's mouth as he found her slit and pushed his tongue between her lower lips.

Her hips bucked up into his face instinctively, seeking pressure where it felt best.

Stratford obliged, hiding nothing of his eagerness to taste her. Win was indeed wonderful on his tongue. He struggled for more, and Win obliged, lifting to help get his head between her legs and her breeches.

With such unfettered access, he lapped hungrily at her folds, and easily found her swollen clitoris. He worked the little peak carefully, bringing her as much excitement as he could manage. Neglected, his own swollen cock had to be satisfied with the weight of his body pressing it against hard ground repeatedly.

But it would have to be enough. Win's pleasure was more important than his own.

He got her legs back up into the air and dived under her garments from a new angle. With such openness, her thighs against his ears, he was back in familiar territory.

He pushed his tongue into her passage a little way, earning a high-pitched gasp and a rush of moisture spilling across his tongue. He probed her again and again and again, and then returned to suck her clitoris in earnest. She would come undone by his mouth and nothing else.

Winston writhed against his face, and Stratford had to hold her hips down, but then she bucked up and screamed out wordlessly, clenching her thighs tight around his head. He rode out the waves of her passion, softening his kisses to her sex as she slowly subsided. When her thighs relaxed enough to release his head, he moved to a more comfortable position at her side and took himself in hand through his breeches. It would only take a few strokes to find his completion after that glorious moment between Win's thighs.

He met her gaze and smiled at the stunned but sated expression on her face. "My dearest, thank you for allowing me the honor of seeing to your satisfaction."

Her lips twitched. "Is that what you say to all the women you debauch on this blanket?"

"Only to the ones posing as a valet," he promised. He pushed the heel of his hand down his length and back up again. "Could I persuade you to lend me a hand now?"

She glanced down, eyes widening at the sight of him stroking himself. Her lips parted as he continued to stroke.

"Are you at all curious to feel what you've lacked between your legs, posing as Winston?"

"I know what you have under there, my lord," she whispered.

"You peeked?"

"I did." She reached out and undid the buttons on the fall of his trousers. "But show me again."

"How kind of you to ask." He pushed the material of his shirt aside and waggled his cock at her playfully. "It's big, isn't it?"

To his delight, Win wet her lips and gulped. "Yes."

"Touch me," he urged, tucking his head close to hers.

Winston's fingers were on him in an instant, and he shuddered, pushing his cock against her hand in want of more of that light touch on his skin. He needed it. Craved her.

Since she was inexperienced, he taught her how to stroke him, showed her what he liked best and then left her to excite him. It did not take long at all for him to reach the point of release. He covered her hand, pointed the tip of his cock down toward the blanket beneath them and together they brought him off.

And when the spasms had passed, he kissed her lips fiercely. He'd never made love to a valet before, but he had to say he liked it very much.

He wanted to do it all again, too. Bring her pleasure with his hands and tongue. Show her all the delights to be found in the bedchamber that she'd denied herself with her ruse.

However, he'd not counted on Winston's competitive nature. When he tried to climb atop her, he ended up under her instead. They tussled for dominance a moment more, rolling all around on the blanket together with their breeches open and laughing about it. Eventually Stratford won, simply by kissing her and then turned her onto her stomach. He pinned her down and planted a kiss on her bare bottom, and then another. "The sweetest bum I've ever seen."

Win struggled and pushed his head away from her rear, attempting to sit up. "My lord, please. Listen! You must stop."

He looked up at her face at last. "What's wrong? I thought you were enjoying that."

"There was a rider coming toward us but now they're galloping away very fast," she warned, her face growing paler by the moment as she fumbled with righting her clothing. "We were seen."

Stratford spun to look beyond win. Far in the distance, he could see a lone rider racing away. He squinted at the figure and realized it was a woman, though he couldn't make out who it was. But the only women who would be riding across the estate should have been a member of his family. "Damn it."

"What do we do?"

Dear God, what they must have imagined they'd seen him and Winston doing on this hill together. He glanced at Winston in horror. Everyone at the palace believed Winston was a man. His reputation would be in tatters. He'd be disgraced if that relation told anyone what she thought she'd seen them doing.

Even the truth, that Winston was a woman, would be a disaster for his continued freedom.

He had to find out who it had been and try to explain or buy them off somehow. "I'll think of something."

"Stratford," Win said slowly. "Perhaps I should just go."

"No. I'll not have it," he said, determined to keep Win at Ravenswood. If he was going to be forced into a marriage he'd rather it be with someone like Win. "You go back to the palace now, and return to your usual routine of being my valet. I'll stay here and paint and return in a few hours as I would normally do as if nothing happened."

She stared at him with a worried expression for so long, he reached out to brush her cheek gently. "We've done nothing wrong."

"I encouraged you. I know what people might think if we were seen together while I was dressed like this. But if they know the truth, it will be just as bad, won't it?"

Clearly, Win had not been lying about her disinterest in matrimony.

"I knew what I was doing too," he promised her. Yet, he was sure he could hear the faint ring of wedding bells in the back of his mind…growing louder by the minute. To his surprise, he wasn't the least bit concerned about the prospect of being leg-shackled.

Chapter Ten

Winston was tense as she entered Ravenswood Palace. Stratford was to blame, of course, not that she regretted the morning outing or falling victim to her own newly awakened curiosity about intimacy between men and women.

Lovemaking was better than she had assumed. So was kissing Lord Stratford. He'd made her surrender less awkward than she feared it might be. It was only after that doubts had surfaced.

The rider racing away was her current concern. She had seen no lady on her long walk back to the palace.

The promise that Lord Stratford would take care of the rider sat oddly on her shoulders. She was not used to leaving others to clean up her messes. The right course of action was to leave before she was identified. Before someone she'd come to care for ended up with their reputation in ruins or married to her instead.

She could always find another position. But husbands and wives were bound together for life. She had known that every acquaintance or friendship she struck up would be as temporary as her time with Lord Stratford surely must be now.

Winston removed her hat as she strode boldly into the Palace and glanced into the cavernous kitchen in the hope of getting a drink. Everyone seemed too busy to notice her at first, scrubbing pots and putting things away.

"You, there. New man," a woman called out.

Winston spun about, looking for the speaker. "Yes?"

The cook, strands of sweaty hair stuck to her brow, emerged from a storeroom, and scowled at Winston. "I know what you're about. Special treatment is for the duke alone."

Winston frowned at the woman and dug a finger into her cravat in a vain attempt to cool herself down. The long walk and accompanying panic had heated her but the kitchen was stifling, too. She set her fingers lightly to the nearest tabletop to steady herself. "Special treatment?"

"Meals are served at nine o'clock, two o'clock and ten o'clock in the evening."

"Yes, I know," Winston sighed, leaning a little harder on the table. "Seymour explained that. I will eat later with everyone here."

The cook's scowl darkened, and she slammed what she was holding onto the table and punched her hands to her hips. "Was the tray Lord Stratford supposedly demanded this morning not enough?"

"What tray? What demand?" Winston shook her head, utterly confused. Perhaps it was the heat but most likely her many exertions that morning that had fatigued her. She needed desperately to sit down a moment and gather her strength. "I've only just returned from a distant hillock. Lord Stratford had the urge to see the sunrise and paint it, and is still there. We left while the palace was still in darkness without eating or requesting any tray. What might be the time, if you don't mind telling me, so I won't miss my luncheon?"

If she did, she might just faint clean away.

The cook's lips pursed tight; her eyes narrowed.

"I would give anything for a sip of water," she said, looking at the cook hopefully, but the woman just stared. "If you will excuse me, I'm truly parched," she explained, wiping her brow before returning the hat to head and turning unsteadily for the nearest exit. There would be water in Lord Stratford's chambers, but she would have to break the rules to drink it. Currently, she did not care.

"Sit," Cook said, and when Winston did not move fast enough, she made it an order. "I said sit while I get you something." She turned and addressed her helpers. "Everyone, there will be no more trays sent upstairs to Lord Stratford's chambers, no matter who says he wants one. Is that clear?"

Winston set her hat next to her on the bench and shook her head. "I never asked for a tray for him. Not once. He eats well with his brothers, he tells me."

"Yes, that is what I thought too," Cook murmured, looking very unhappy. "But someone has been requesting them for Lord Stratford and eating the contents of those trays. I assumed it was you but you look about ready to faint from hunger. I cannot abide dishonesty in our ranks."

The cook disappeared into the larder.

Winston put her elbows on the battered wood table and rested there, wondering about the trays that had never come to her attention in Lord Stratford's room. Was someone stealing food in her name? That's a fine way to get handed your marching orders in such a strict household. She wondered who would be so brazen and then dismissed the matter. She was much too tired and hungry to care.

When Cook emerged, she plonked down a jug of water and a glass, which Winston snatched up. She drank two glasses of water by the time the cook returned with cheese, a half loaf of bread and a leg of ham covered in cloth. She set everything on the table in front of Winston and produced a long sharp knife from under her apron to carve off two thick slices of each. "I'll not be made a fool of in my own kitchen."

"I don't understand. What's been going on?"

The cook laid a hand on Winston's shoulder. "Never you mind, lovey. I'll deal with the troublemaker in our midst, never fear. Now go on.

Eat. I suspect you've not had a proper meal since you got here."

Winston had not, but did not complain. She was ravenous, no doubt from her recent exertions that morning. Keeping up with Lord Stratford while burdened had been a strain. Her legs had not felt at all steady after she'd made love to him, either. She dipped her chin to hide a blush at her behavior and tucked into the veritable feast before her, gulping down the milk the cook also set down in front of her as well.

She wiped her mouth with the sleeve of her coat. "Thank you, madam."

"The name's Mrs. Derry. Mr. Seymour was no doubt too busy to arrange a proper introduction when you first arrived."

"I'm sure he never meant to slight you," Winston promised, hoping that was true.

"With all the shenanigans going on around here, the dozens of visiting servants getting in the way, contradicting everything, I'm sure he didn't mean to slight you, either. But you're more important than all the new faces to me. You belong to the palace now. I've always had a soft spot for Lord Stratford's valets. You've got your work cut out for you keeping him on time," she said, blushing a little. "How he keeps any manservants, I'll never know."

Winston smiled, remembering how exasperating the man could really be. Clearly, despite his flaws, Stratford was universally adored.

Winston just hoped she'd not gone and ruined that for him.

She ate her fill and then excused herself from the cook.

"We take care of our own, below stairs. Whatever nonsense is going on upstairs should not affect you again," Mrs. Derry promised, and then cocked her head, clearly listening. "You run along now, it's about to get busy again."

Winston heard the rush of feet and turned for the hall. Footmen and maids flooded into the hallway from all directions ahead of her. They were rushing for the front of the house, which meant someone else was arriving at the palace. Winston was swept along with them into a servants-only passageway but managed to step into a man-sized niche in the wall just before she reached the front hall, where the activity was at its most frenetic.

From this vantage point, she could see the library was located directly opposite her position. A traveling carriage could be seen through the open doorway and palace footmen were filing out to receive the guests. The maids peeked through the front hall windows and then headed back the way they'd come. "No ladies in the carriage. Only men again this time," Nan remarked, clearly disappointed, as they passed Winston by headed back to the servants' hall. "Did you hear who it was?"

"I heard the butler say it was no one the duke

could have invited," Milly told her. "That list was complete days ago."

Winston became curious about the uninvited guests and held her spot a moment before deciding she would have a better view from within the library. She could always dust something if questioned about why she was there.

The front hall was momentarily empty, and Winston moved swiftly, slipping across the parquetry floor, and ducking inside the library undetected. There was no one there at the moment, so she pushed the door shut in the hope it might stay that way. From the library front window, she glimpsed a fine black traveling carriage and a large young man emerging to be greeted by the palace butler, Seymour. The uninvited guest seemed young and obviously well-off, judging by the quality of his greatcoat and the shine on his boots. Given the way he looked down his nose at the butler, he was clearly part of higher society.

Winston drew back, deciding there was nothing more out there to interest her and turned to take in the room. The duke's library was massive, the largest she'd ever dreamed could exist. Books were stacked to the roof upon shelves and piled high on other surfaces, too.

If Winston were younger, and not a servant, she'd want nothing more than to stay in this room forever, reading every single volume. Learning from pages instead of out there in the world was a damn sight easier.

She scouted the room, looking for anything that might give a clue as to where books on the peerage might be found. She found one such volume resting upon a walnut lectern, open as if it had just been perused. Taking special care to note the exact page, she flicked back to the front to look up her own ancestors. Her father had not been titled but they were distantly connected to a duke, and she had once been called upon to recite those ancestors names by heart.

Her father had been so proud his own name had been listed in such an important book, along with his wife's and his son.

Winston ran her finger down the entries until she found her father, Mr. Edwin Joseph Aston. Married to Josephine Taylor. Their son, Edwin Neil Aston, born eight years after they married. But there was no mention of any deaths.

Winston flicked to the front of the volume to look at the year of printing, assuming it must be an old edition not to have the deaths recorded.

"This year's edition," she whispered to herself. "That should have been enough time."

Mama had drowned in the carriage accident that had separated Winston from her father. Clearly, the news of the younger Edwin Aston's demise had also failed to reach the publishers for this edition, too. But it had been ten years since the accident. The day she'd run away from everything she'd ever known, hoping Father would assume she had perished in the river along with Mama. Father must not have sent the notices.

There was no telling why he hadn't done so. He should have been glad to be rid of her and mama, too.

She put the volume back exactly as she had found it, open to the right place, and headed for the library doors. But once there, she heard voices in the entrance hall and froze with her hand on the knob. Carefully, she put her eye to the crack and, seeing nothing on the other side, slowly eased the door open a tiny bit to see who was there.

The first thing she saw was the expanse of a gentleman's expensive black great coat. The man she had seen standing beside the carriage out front, talking with Seymour.

"I shall want an audience as soon as he returns," an old man said, his voice rasping over her entire body and giving her an unexpected shock.

Winston knew that voice.

Had known it as well as her own once.

She drew back, gulped, and then quickly put her eye back to the gap again, hoping she was mistaken.

The large form of the younger new arrival blocked her view of the hall entirely.

"Of course, sir. It shall be an honor to arrange an interview," Seymour promised him.

"See that you do. Come along, son."

Winston snapped to attention and had to firm her grip on the door handle to hold herself in place. She had instinctively wanted to obey that old man's voice.

Her father's voice.

The fellow blocking her view suddenly stepped away—and Winston was looking directly into the face of her own personal nightmare. She froze, standing there watching a man she'd hoped never to see again through the small opening in the door. He was much older, but she'd know that face anywhere.

Her father was right there in front of her.

But he turned for the distant public rooms with that other man following after him.

The man Father had called son.

Winston frowned but watched until the doors to the other room were pulled shut behind them. Still, she could not move a muscle.

She had a father still...and apparently a brother now, too.

Father must have remarried quickly after Mama's death to have such a large offspring. Winston was four and twenty. That young man shouldn't be more than ten years old at most.

And yet father called him son.

She looked back at the lectern and the book laying open upon it. There had been no mention of any second married for her father in the records she'd just read. That seemed unusual, too. It was the current edition.

Winston put her hand to her throat and backed away from the door, taking deep breaths and struggling to control her confusion. It was not turning out to be a very good day at all. She'd been seen with Lord Stratford, and now her father would be a guest under the same roof as herself. So close but as yet unaware of his firstborn's presence. It worried her that her father was familiar enough with the Duke of Ravenswood to demand an interview immediately upon his arrival. He hadn't even been invited to come.

She returned to the copy of the peerage and again read the published date of that volume. It was just as she remembered. Father would have ensured any second marriage of his and the birth of a second heir, an actual son, had been recorded and published for all to see.

Only one thing was clear though—she had to get away from Ravenswood Palace. She wasn't safe. No matter how much she wanted to believe the past no longer mattered, it had finally found her.

She was supposed to be dead.

Winston waited until the hall was quiet and then fled up the main staircase and along to the dubious safety of Lord Stratford's bedchamber, where she hid in his dressing closet for a full hour, shaking uncontrollably. When her panic passed, she gathered up her few personal possessions and held them tightly to her chest. She felt bad about abandoning her post at a difficult time for Lord Stratford. She must leave, without saying goodbye, too, at first light tomorrow, and without the generous wages he'd promised to pay her.

She would miss their conversations, and his kisses. But if Stratford knew her father, she and the lord should never have even met.

Chapter Eleven

Assuming Win's return to the house had passed without incident, Stratford prowled the lower levels of the palace as if he wasn't in an utter panic. He had already handed off his canvas, paints, and easel to the first footman he'd seen and looked around again, wondering where Win might be found now.

He saw a number of family members sitting in pockets enjoying the delights of Ravenswood Palace in the morning. None called out to him or followed to ask to speak with him, privately or otherwise. Yet someone staying at the manor had seen him and Win making love out there on the grounds. A someone who could make his life difficult if they cared to.

He had assumed the rider, and anyone else they'd told, would be waiting to accuse him of committing the crime of making love with another man. That was a hanging offense. But no one seemed lurking in wait for him yet. After engaging in brief conversations with anyone he did see, he quickly moved on from each group slightly relieved, but the tension was mounting inside him.

The list of possibilities was growing shorter by the minute.

The long gallery doors were open to enjoy the views and was full of guests, cousins all, but an accuser was nowhere to be found among those standing around gossiping. In the dining room, he saw Crawford and Cousin Amity sitting together near the more open terrace doors, taking tea a little apart from everyone else, and he quickly went to join them.

"Good morning to you both," he murmured, taking a seat beside Amity and smiling at her... but she did not smile in return.

His stomach pitted. Amity looked happier yesterday. Had she been out riding this morning? She asked nothing about his whereabout that morning and let her husband fill the void with chatter.

Yet, even as he conversed with Crawford, he felt something was off about Amity today. She was too quiet, but he hoped he was wrong that she might have seen him and Winston together and misunderstood.

He glanced around, uncomfortable with his conclusions. He hadn't wanted to tell anyone about Winston. Not yet. Not when he was finally getting somewhere with the stubborn woman.

Amity caught his eye again, gave him a half smile and leaned closer. "I did not see you at dinner last night."

"I went to bed early," he told her. And that

was the truth but had not been his intention at the time. The wine and company had lulled him into sleep better than any medicinal draft Nash had ever concocted for him over the years. "Slept like a log."

Her brow rose. "Alone?"

"Of course," he promised.

Stratford had enjoyed making Winston laugh last night. The wine and good company had mellowed the usually straight-faced valet. It was no surprise she'd always been so serious all the time. She must have known any levity would have revealed the prettiness of her features. Her musical laughter, too, was a delight for its rarity. He hoped to hear more of it in due time.

The country walk they'd taken this morning, while enjoyable, had revealed the unexpected dangers of seducing a woman wearing men's clothing though. Yet the idea of escaping again with Win was definitely appealing, going somewhere private where they could let their curiosity take them anywhere they dared.

He'd crossed a line but was committed to never returning to the way things had been. Win could not be his valet, although he would allow her to undertake some of those duties until they could leave Ravenswood Palace together. If she did nothing, it would be noticed by other servants.

He glanced around, and his tension returned. One of these people must have seen him. What were they waiting for?

Yet each and every one smiled at him in turn, and otherwise showed no sign of revulsion or interest when meeting his gaze. Except for Cousin George, who wore a perpetual scowl as he looked across the gallery at his newly married sister, husband, and himself.

Amity cleared her throat. "Might I trouble you for a private conversation?"

"Yes, of course, cousin. I'd be more than happy to speak with you, and your husband too." However, at that moment, an unexpected figure strode into the room. Mr. Edwin Aston Senior, followed by his much larger son, Edwin.

He turned quickly to Amity and lowered his voice. "When the hell did Aston arrive?"

"Not that long ago. Why?"

"He wasn't expected," he muttered. The duke was away from the estate, along with his brothers, on business in the nearest village this morning. They would not be pleased to find Aston had arrived while they were gone. Undoubtedly this was George's doing, bringing Aston to the estate now.

He glanced at George and saw a smirk on his face—confirmation Aston was part of his plan to cause Ravenswood trouble.

"Has Aston met with the duke yet?"

"I shouldn't think so. Ravenswood left at dawn with your brothers. Why?"

Ravenswood owed Aston the most of anyone.

There was not enough money in the collective pool yet to cover that particular debt by half. Seeing him in conversation with George Sweet made him wonder if his cousin somehow knew the estate was in financial trouble. "Just keeping abreast of current events," he promised Amity, though his eyes returned to George.

It was hard to tell what George Sweet knew at any one time, but he was clearly enjoying acting the generous host today and making it seem he had the ear of the current duke. He'd always been the jealous sort, especially toward Algernon, and spiteful to everyone else. When he embraced young Edwin Aston, Stratford's stomach soured even more.

Stratford had once wanted to be Edwin's friend.

Seeing the friendly exchange with George made him glad they hardly ever had occasion to be in each other's company these days.

Young Edwin Aston was a big man, barrel-chested and robust, but with eyes so bloodshot from excessive drinking they sometimes seemed to be burning. He lived a life of excess and belligerence, much like George.

The elder Aston was a smaller man, wiry in form. Stratford did not know him at all well, so he studied the way he behaved with Cousin George, storing up the information to relay to his brother later. Aston spoke quietly with authority, suggesting he was a man in control of his emotions at all times. Quite the opposite to his old friend, Stratford's late father.

But they had been the best of friends for ages, since before Stratford had even been born. Why else would he loan Father so much money over the years?

Stratford dug his finger under his collar. Aston was the last complication they needed this week.

He noted a few cousins push their chairs back to greet the newcomers, and young Edwin Aston was drawn away with them. Stratford would undoubtedly have to speak with Edwin later in the day, but he was not in a rush to do so. The few times their paths had crossed in society in recent years, it had seemed Edwin preferred not to remember the time they'd spent together as children.

That had stung.

It wasn't often Stratford was confronted by an acquaintance who ignored him. But Edwin had changed too much since they were boys, playing together on the Aston estate, for him to regret it now. Edwin Aston was a connection, a friendship, he would never want to resurrect.

George Sweet followed after Edwin, calling to him to wait.

With the room emptier, Stratford stood and approached Mr. Aston with his hand extended. "Good morning, sir," he exclaimed. "We are so pleased you could join us this year."

With such a loud remark, how could Aston

refuse to admit to similar pleasure at being at Ravenswood once more? But he remained silent, and their exchange quickly became awkward. The elder Aston wasn't given for small talk, it seemed.

On the previous occasions they'd encountered each other, Aston had focused his attention on Stratford's late father and no one else. With Father gone, and the family still in mourning, he seemed a little distant, but he supposed that was to be expected after losing a long-held friendship.

Stratford decided he should try a little harder to engage him in chatter. But a footman interrupted and offered to fetch the man coffee, and then a selection of delicacies from the sideboard. Stratford bided his time as Aston studied the plate of food and made his choices with careful consideration.

Eventually he caught Aston's eye. "I trust you had a pleasant journey?"

"Indeed, we did," he promised.

"Will you be joining us for the early morning shoot tomorrow?"

"Alas, my eyes are not as they once were and prevent me from enjoying my favorite country pursuits." Aston pushed his coddled eggs around on his plate and then gave up. "But I'm sure my son will join you."

"Wonderful, though I am sorry the duke will not have your company tomorrow. I'm also sorry to say he is away from the estate, and I've no idea exactly when he might return."

"Yes, your cousin said he left the estate unexpectedly."

"Not unexpected at all. A meeting with local merchants was arranged last week for this very morning," Stratford promised, making sure the man had the correct information rather than Cousin George's lies.

Aston's expression grew thoughtful, and he said no more.

Since Aston did not seem inclined to converse, and requested the newssheet, Stratford excused himself to lead Amity from the room. As they crossed the threshold, he overheard Aston strike up a conversation with Crawford, asking where the duke had gone that morning.

Since Crawford likely did not know the exact particulars of the duke's schedule, he wouldn't get much out of Stratford's friend.

Amity walked with him through the gardens, taking him a good distance away from the palace before she spoke. "I am so glad to be married to your friend," she whispered, even though no one was around to hear them. "George is angry and has glared daggers at me since our arrival but my husband glares right back. George doesn't dare say anything too unkind, though I know too well what things he's likely thinking about our surprise marriage. But I am married and beyond his reach, or the brunt of his anger."

"I dare say it's Crawford's untapped bank

account and the duke's public support that have stilled his tongue for now," Stratford replied.

"Speaking of tongues, what is going on with you?"

"Nothing."

"You know exactly what I mean. There was a lady in your chambers last night. Promise me you're not secretly courting one of our cousins."

He nearly choked. "Good God, no. That would be utterly revolting." He shuddered. "Imagine. No!"

"I know what I heard, Stratford. You had a giggling woman in your chambers last night. I've never known you to corrupt a maid, so it must be someone in the family. There is no one else here for you to seduce." She wet her lips. "And then this morning, I saw you with a woman out on the grounds, too."

Stratford's knees nearly buckled. Amity had seen him with a woman. Not a man. Not a servant. Just a woman. There'd be no scandal if he played this right.

"I certainly have not done so, nor ever will seduce a maid or cousin," he promised. "Oh, but my valet was there in my rooms last night, so I suppose you might have heard him laughing at one of my jests."

Amity leaned a little closer. "Cuthbert's laugh is not that high."

"I have a replacement. A young fellow who I suspect has lied about his age now. You mustn't have heard Cuthbert was injured on the way home."

"Oh, I'm sorry to hear that."

"There's of course no woman here I would invite into my chambers," he assured Amity. "I plan to be a bachelor forever, Mrs. Crawford."

"That's what my husband said too once," she murmured. "His heart and soul belong to me now, or so he claims."

"I should certainly hope so," he grinned.

It relieved him no end that Amity might have been too far away to discern what Winston had been wearing this morning. They had been rolling around on the ground at the time Winston had mentioned seeing the rider. "If I were meeting with a woman, and I am not saying I was, she wouldn't be anyone you need to worry yourself about."

Amity gave him a long hard look, and Stratford faced her scrutiny unflinching. He might still be tempted to seduce his current valet, but he would be more circumspect about how he went about it in the future.

However, that would only happen if Win wanted to make love again. They had not had a chance to discuss where their affair was headed. They had parted in a panic. But a woman living as a man might not care to continue an affair with him at all.

It was obvious she had never been kissed before. Stratford had certainly surprised himself by doing so that morning. Then, when offered the chance, he'd acted on instinct to make love out in the open.

Yet, having kissed Winston once, he was looking forward to another opportunity should it come his way again.

Amity linked her arm through his suddenly. "Then what is the reason for the tension I feel between you and your brothers? Always whispering, circling each other about the rooms. That is not at all usual. You're all so serious now, when I know for a fact that deep down you must all be glad Algernon is the duke. Believe me, I am. You should be overjoyed, but you all look worried when around each other. I am certain George has caught the scent of a potential secret in the air, too." She looked at him suddenly, and her eyes widened. "He's not ill, is he? Algernon, I mean."

As much as he liked Amity, there were things he didn't have leave to speak of openly. To do so might bring disaster down on his brothers' hastily made plans. Amity was better off not knowing the details yet, but of course, the secret couldn't be kept forever.

"My brothers are all in the best of health, and if any were ill, you know Nash would have us locked inside our chambers, insisting we're bled and forcing us to sip broth instead of the late duke's wine. There is, of course, a great deal of discussion about the future going on between us brothers. When to end our mourning, returning to London and the season. He needs an heir one day, but Algernon has no real wish to marry," he said, giving the only possible explanation that would not raise more questions. "You know his nature."

"I thought I did, but he's been full of surprises of late. Look, Roman might not seem family to you yet, but he was your friend before we married. If you've gotten yourself into some sort of trouble, he would want to know and would certainly offer his help."

Crawford was now family, and Stratford trusted him with his life, and his cousin's heart. But the state of the duchy was not Stratford's secret to share. He might need to speak to the new duke and warn him that Amity was asking questions. If the Crawfords could be brought into the secret and safely keep their mouths shut, they would have another pair of allies they could turn to for advice and occasional assistance in deflecting the curiosity of others. Certainly, both were determined to thwart Cousin George at every turn.

He nodded. "Crawford is a good man."

"The very best." Amity sighed. The sound of a woman smitten with her love and her marriage. It was what he'd hoped for her but hadn't counted on. To be far away from Cousin George and his unkind influence was another desire, too.

"Tell me, how goes the quest to purchase Uncle Henry's estate?"

"Crawford told you about that already?"

"No. Uncle Henry did. He asked my opinion yesterday. Wondered if Algernon might disapprove of the sale."

"And?"

"I'm sure my brother would rather Crawford buy it than George simply move in. Your brother is known to covet the place."

"For its proximity to Ravenswood and the duke's ear. You must know he has ambitions far beyond what he deserves."

"What he gets will always be far less than he expects," Stratford replied gleefully. There simply was no money for handouts to anyone now, deserving or otherwise.

"He'll cause trouble," Amity warned.

"Hasn't he always tried?"

"I would wager he's not so easily dissuaded now. Did you see how excited he was by Aston's arrival? Something is going on there."

"He's simply grown closer to Edwin," he agreed. "It doesn't matter. Our father found George amusing once. Algernon never will." He patted her hand as he spotted Crawford striding across the lawn to meet them. "Do not worry yourself over nothing, cousin, for here is your husband bounding our way to sweep you off your feet again."

She turned immediately to view her husband. They rushed together and, true to Stratford's prediction, Crawford lifted his bride off the ground and spun her until she giggled and begged to be put down again. The sound reminded him of Winston last night and this morning. Her musical laugh was a memory he already treasured.

He looked up at the facade of Ravenswood Palace and saw her standing at the window of his bedchamber. He almost raised his hand to signal to her but then he saw Mr. Aston, his son, and Cousin George were outside and headed toward the stables, and thought better of it. Winston must have noticed them too, because she drew back, making herself almost undetectable.

She must be so worried she'd be identified as his lover of the morning.

Stratford excused himself and conjured a feeble excuse to return to his room and tell her it was all right now.

Chapter Twelve

W inston moved swiftly down the hall, one eye open for any lurkers until she reached a door she shouldn't want to open as much as she currently did. She pressed her ear to the door to listen for any movement inside and, upon hearing nothing, silently let herself inside.

The first thing that assailed her was the scent she had nearly forgotten but had once meant so much to her. Pipe smoke mixed with strong sandalwood cologne.

The memories of her lost childhood hit her like a blow, painful and unwanted, and she cursed under her breath. Now was not the time to become foolishly sentimental.

Winston hurried to the windows facing the stables and cautiously peered out. She saw the man who had sired her, in conversation with the stable master, along with a few other gentlemen. His son was one, and a man dressed all in black— George Sweet, she assumed—as they looked over the horses.

Believing that her father might be there a good while, she turned to view the guest chamber and studied her surroundings.

Aston appeared to travel as lightly as he always

had. The well-worn traveling cases were stacked neatly at the foot of the bed. His hairbrush and shaving implements were placed on the dresser near a full-length mirror.

As she turned around, she caught sight of a thin book lying on a table beside the only comfortable chair in the room. It was obviously well-handled. The cover worn and soiled, the edges of the paper yellowed and stained. She considered taking a peek at what might have been inside but then decided against it. She wasn't part of his world anymore. She did not have to be better educated than her father, as he had once insisted she must be, to bring the family the distinction he craved and to make him proud. Aston had a real son to fulfill that longing of his now.

She pressed her lips together and shook her head. There was no point regretting her failures. She could not change her gender to please him or anyone.

Aware time was passing, she started for the door but stopped beside the bed when she saw a small, stoppered vial. It was the kind given out by apothecaries for a variety of ailments. She picked up the bottle to study the contents and then held it up to the light. It contained a fine white powder but there was no label to explain what it was meant to cure.

Winston put the bottle back down quickly, making sure she left it exactly as she had found it.

But she frowned a moment. Was her father ill? She'd never known him to be in anything but in the best of health. But he was getting older, and she didn't know what had happened in his life since she'd last seen him.

Saddened by that, she headed for the door and an escape, slipping into the empty hall and hurrying back the way she'd come without trying to show how much she wished to run. As she reached Lord Stratford's chamber door and turned the handle, she heard the thump of heavy steps behind her and glanced over her shoulder.

Father was farther down the hall, shuffling toward his guest room.

A shiver raced over her skin to be even this close to him again, and the fear that he'd notice her grew. She tightened her grip on the handle and opened the door silently, determined not to fall victim to her misplaced emotions and be discovered. The father she'd respected, adored, had wanted her dead once, after all.

She could never forget that, or trust that he could have forgotten what she was.

But watching him now, she saw he limped the whole way to his door, and as he reached for the handle of his guest room, she thought she heard him sigh in pain.

She leaned toward the sound, straining to hear him again.

But he straightened instantly, and as his head started to turn in her direction, perhaps aware that he wasn't alone, Winston finally stepped into Lord Stratford's room.

"What were you looking at?" Lord Stratford asked in a tone so unexpected, she jumped almost out of her skin.

Winston shut the door behind her. "Nothing."

"Really? You had such an odd look on your face," he murmured, getting to his feet, and trying to look past her. "George wasn't lurking out there, was he?"

"I don't believe so." Winston made sure the door was firmly closed behind her, locking it for good measure. "It must have been your imagination."

Stratford frowned at her. "Where were you just then?"

"The servants' hall," she said, moving away from the door.

Lord Stratford followed. "No, you were just here at the window. In this room, and then gone by the time I got here. It's not been long enough for you to visit the servants' hall and return in that time. I know. I timed the journey once when I was younger."

"Why?"

"I wanted to know I could raid the larder and get back before one of my brothers noticed I was gone. I managed to make such a habit of it that Cook began leaving me a plate of biscuits on the kitchen table so I could cut down the time."

She forced a smile. "I am quick on my feet, just like you."

"No one is that quick."

She shrugged, wishing he would stop pestering her about her movements. "Did you need something, my lord?"

"I saw you peeking out the window. You were watching me," he murmured, a smug smile growing on his lips.

"So what if I was?" she said quickly, raising her chin in defiance. It had been reckless to watch her employer and definitely wrong of her to go to her father's room just now. She didn't really know why she'd gone or what she had hoped to find there. All she felt now was profound sadness when she thought of his solitary figure moving down the hall. She did not think him happy, not that he'd ever been a joyous man during her youth, either.

"I am glad you wanted to watch me." Stratford eased forward a step and a look of concern appeared on his face. "How do you feel? Do you regret what we did this morning?"

"No. Did you expect me to?"

"I certainly hope not." Stratford gestured to her. "Come closer."

"Why?"

"Just come closer, Win. The time for distance and maidenly reserve is well in the past now."

Winston agreed and moved the last step toward him. He reached for her face, and Winston assumed he meant to pull her in for a kiss. A kiss she was looking forward to experiencing again.

However, he only brushed his thumb across her cheek. He held it up for her to see. "A tear."

Winston brushed at her face quickly, confused, and embarrassed. "There must have been something in my eye."

"Are you sure that's all it was?" he asked, and then pulled her into his arms and held her hips pressed tight against his. "It's all right to regret the partial loss of your innocence."

She didn't know why he felt the need to comfort her about that until she pulled in a deep breath to deny any such regret, and it ended in a sob. Ordinarily, she did not cry. That was a sign of weakness in men, and a tactic used by women to manipulate their husbands.

But in that moment, with Stratford holding her, Winston couldn't stop.

She missed her father.

She turned her face down so Stratford couldn't see as the tears continued to fall down her cheeks. She put her hands over her face, too, and Stratford held her close.

"Don't worry about the state of my coat. My temporary almost-valet will fix it later," he whispered.

That made her laugh, and she drew back from him, giving her eyes one last wipe with the back of her hand. "Yes, you're very lucky indeed to have someone as patient as me."

"I am lucky," he promised, putting his hand on his heart. "I know that. I would have been very late for every luncheon or dinner and my brother would have been so cross. I do not regret being made a fool, either."

That brought a blush to her cheeks, and she turned away from him. "Did you come up here for a reason?"

"Yes," he admitted, then sighed heavily. "I know who saw us. She won't say anything about the woman I made love to this morning."

Winston sagged. "Good."

He came up behind her, rubbing her arms. "It's not the same as it was between us now."

"No, I suppose it isn't."

"I want more," he said. "I feel a little desperate when I see you, and when I can't find you, I experience fear you'll disappear."

She turned slowly and looked up at him, wondering if he knew she was going. "Why?"

"I…" he began. "I can't explain it. I just know this cannot continue, but while it does, I don't want to waste a moment with you."

But she suddenly wished it could continue. She enjoyed dressing him and bossing him about. Then there was that lustful look in his eye right now that spoke of hunger and mischief. He looked at her, now he knew her secret, and she desperately wanted to throw caution to the wind and stay.

It was foolish to feel anything for someone she

hardly knew but she might now understand those maids and their giggling obsession with the scandalous Sweet brothers. Hers was the best man she'd ever gotten to know.

A tiny thrill swept over her that she could not suppress at the pleasure she'd found in taking this position. Stratford was the first man she found attractive who had ever regarded her as a desirable woman. That eager consideration on his part was new and something she cherished.

She was not pretty in this guise, and yet, Stratford seemed to find something in her current appearance that intrigued him and drew him close. For her part, she had a great curiosity to learn what it might be.

She exhaled slowly, admitting to the one flaw in her nature that she'd never be able to escape. She craved approval. Yearned for affection after so long without. A younger brother of a duke could not keep a woman like her around, someone who dressed as a man, as his lover forever.

But luckily, Winston had never really believed in forever.

Right now was all she might ever have with him.

The desire to learn what it truly meant to be a woman, and be made love to, suddenly consumed her thoughts, and she turned around to be in his arms. There was no one better suited to teach her the intricacies of lovemaking than the one man she'd never meant to reveal her nature too.

She looked up at him now and a blush warmed her skin as she remembered the way they had been that morning. She'd no idea what to do about the unwanted emotions being around him seemed to draw out of her, other than to act on them.

Thankfully, he was just as willing.

He reached for her face again, drew her closer and gently set his lips to hers. There was once again that strange surge of energy between them, drawing her deeper into his arms and further into their kiss, without her even thinking about it. His fingers cradled her skull as he bent over her.

She opened her eyes and saw his were closed. She shut hers quickly, assuming that was the way it should be done.

After a moment, he drew back, panting. "Winston…we should not do this again."

His kisses were so drugging that for a moment, she didn't understand him. But when she did, she was struck by acute embarrassment and humiliation. "I'm sorry."

He grasped her arm tightly. "I shouldn't want to kiss you when you're dressed like that."

She glanced down. They were dressed much the same. They always had been. Breeches, stockings, and waistcoat. And all the usual embellishments of a gentleman, although his garments were of richer quality. She could understand his hesitation. It might seem at first like he was kissing another man even now. Which is how she would always appear to him, wearing her disguise. But he clearly enjoyed being around beautiful women wearing scandalous red dresses, and perhaps nothing at all, too.

There was a time and place to let down her guard. This was that moment. Tomorrow, she'd be gone. She would never have this chance again to be how she'd been born. "Undress me."

"Winston," he said in a tone that sounded like a warning.

"I mean it. I want to be kissed by you, and if removing my garments is the only way you can feel comfortable doing so again, well..." She shrugged, her stomach quaking. "It must be done."

He chuckled softly. "I said I shouldn't kiss you when you look like me, not that I wouldn't want to."

He pulled her tighter into his arms, driving her backward toward his large bed. She could feel his hands on her back where they lingered over the bindings around her chest. Men seem inordinately obsessed with breasts, she'd noticed. And suddenly she wanted to be free of restrictions, to feel Stratford's hands and lips on her breasts to discover what all the fuss was about.

Winston fumbled with the buttons on her waistcoat.

"Wait," Stratford whispered. "The door."

"Locked already," she assured him.

He groaned and ran his hands up and down

her back briskly. "You definitely are my kind of woman."

"Don't call me that," she hissed, nearly dancing in her eagerness to get on with their seduction of each other.

He chuckled softly in her ear and then kissed it. "Do you object to compliments, Win?"

"The compliment is fine, but the description is problematic, given I'm wearing the guise of your valet."

"You are a woman in all the places that count to me," he assured her. His hips pressed against hers, and she felt his arousal prodding her. "In a moment, you won't be wearing any clothing, only a smile as luminous as your wore at sunrise."

Sunrise with a man between her legs, making her squirm and cry out in pleasure with his tongue lapping at her. Now she would be bare in his arms, with no barriers left between them at all. No modesty, no impediments to any lovemaking. She wanted that—and yet she had a moment of doubt. Lovemaking frequently led to child-making. Winston could not leave Stratford, only to discover later that she'd become pregnant by him. She'd not be able to live as a gentleman then and earn her way in the world. A rounded belly wouldn't fool anyone much beyond a fleeting glimpse.

She put her hand on his chest. Holding him back momentarily, trying to work out how to tell him.

"Just kisses again," he promised in a whisper. "We'll lie together on my bed and explore each other fully with only with our hands and lips and tongues. I'm not ready for fatherhood, either."

She nodded quickly, grateful he'd understood her hesitation and felt the same. It wasn't as if she wasn't curious about everything possible between a man and woman now. That morning's lovemaking had been divine until the moment she'd feared they'd been seen. There had also been a furtiveness about their lack of undressing, too.

She moved to undo one button on her waistcoat, but Stratford's hand covered hers. Holding her still. "Let's not rush this moment of surrender."

She nodded and relaxed even more into his embrace. Stratford knew what he was doing, and he also knew how inexperienced she really was. She'd only just had her first climax after all, thanks to him.

She gave herself up to wherever her emotions took her. He helped her out of her coat and urged her to lay down with her head on his pillow.

She watched him remove his coat and for a change, he carefully laid it across the back of a chair. His waistcoat and shirt ended up there neatly, too, and that amused her. "I appreciate you not making more work for me later."

His smile was immediate. "I aim to please."

"You do. Please me, I mean. As a lover. As an

employer, however, you can be rather frustrating," she told him.

"Deliberately, to get a rise out of you," he whispered, grinning despite her criticism. He sat beside her hip and captured her fingers. "We will have to be cautious carrying on our affair," he whispered.

"I understand," she whispered back, but there would be no continuation tomorrow.

"It will be easier when we return to London together," he promised.

She looked at him in shock. "London?"

"There are fewer people in Ravenswood House, and far more opportunities for us to have fun together elsewhere, too. There are any number of scandalous places two gentlemen might visit together after dark and no one will think twice about it."

Winston stilled momentarily. Stratford spoke of a long future as her lover, but that could not be. Even a future that promised the continuation of the pleasures she was only just discovering could never be considered. Her father was just down the hall. "We can discuss it later."

"Yes," he said, leaning over her. "We will have all the time in the world soon."

Winston looped her arms around his neck and pulled him down for a kiss. But it was mainly to hide the sadness she experienced over the thought of leaving him. Tomorrow, he'd wake up alone and have to tie his own cravat and pick up his own clothes...or he'd stand before the easel all day, painting in ignorance.

Hopefully, by the time he realized she was gone, she would be miles away. Far beyond his reach, and that of her father, too.

Now she knew what to do with a man's body, she brushed her fingers down his bare chest until she encountered his bulging trousers.

He broke the kiss, chuckling. "You are a fast learner."

"I had a good teacher."

"My dear, your lessons are only just getting started," he promised as he rolled her fully under him.

She shook her head. Lord, he could talk. "Stratford, shut up and kiss me."

Chapter Thirteen

S tratford marveled at the ridiculousness of his cousin George's babble the next morning. While everyone prowled forward through the long grass in near silence, George, of course, chose to do the exact opposite. Even Stratford knew shooting required one to shut their mouth or risk scaring off the wildlife. He glared at George, who was leaning against young Edwin Aston, explaining some past shoot where he'd brought down the greater number of birds and earned praise from the late duke.

It had been a long morning of him boasting and drinking with Edwin Aston. They never stopped, and they were a distraction the shooting party could frankly do without.

He glanced at the duke in exasperation. Why was Algernon putting up with this nonsense?

Surely it was time to put their cousin in his place.

He handed off his gun to one of the servants in frustration and stalked over to his brother, who was standing near a collection of woven baskets.

"We're short a few birds still," Algernon was saying to Crawford, who was raising his new rifle and taking aim at a cloud above them. "I'll not go back yet."

"I think we ought to leave them out here to get the rest," Stratford muttered softly, not bothering to hide his annoyance.

Algernon smiled. "I might be tempted to do the same. However, I looked at the tally. His prowess is far below standard."

"That has always been the case," Stratford murmured.

"But it isn't what our cousin has achieved in the past that matters anymore," Algernon answered and finally looked up, grinning. "It is what he can do from today that we will dine on at gatherings in the future."

"Ah, of course," Stratford said, finally understanding why Algernon wasn't annoyed. George tended to bludgeon everyone with his self-praise, but Algernon had always played a game of subtlety. Only a fool would believe George's boasts when there was no one important enough, such as the late duke, to support his version of his achievements.

Stratford retrieved his gun and moved forward with his brothers and, at a signal, took aim. He had a near miss for one bird, but the duke's aim was better. To the left, there was no sound of a gunshot but the harsh braying of drunken laughter.

Stratford did not bother to turn and look. George and Aston hadn't taken a single shot.

Algernon signaled they were done for the day, and George and Aston wasted no time leading the way back to the palace. That was where the rum and any other spirits were to be found, after all.

Stratford joined his brothers to watch them stumble off together.

"Not so much as a by your leave," Jasper complained.

"They barely acknowledged the duke all morning," Nash complained. "It's as if he imagines nothing has changed."

Algernon said nothing to that. But his lips pursed in thought.

Stratford clapped his hand on the duke's shoulder. "What's next?"

"Next?"

"In your plan to humiliate George. After all the slights you suffered over the years, I imagine you have endless plans?"

"I wouldn't waste my energy on so poor a target. His soft spots are rather obvious after all."

Stratford frowned. "Not to me."

Algernon leaned close. "The man adores his wife, even though she obviously loathes him still. He'd do anything to win her favor. If I wanted to cause trouble for him, all I'd have to do is befriend his bride. Melody Sweet quite obviously wants nothing more than to be important to the family, the center of attention, and a leader of our little society. The one everyone turns to in these difficult times. George alone cannot give her that."

"No, he cannot," Stratford murmured, and then he chuckled evilly. "I can't wait to see him try and fail."

"She won't wait for his excuses. Melody has already offered to act as my hostess, for instance, during the season."

Stratford choked. "Please don't allow that."

"I cannot, of course, as I had already asked Mrs. Crawford to do the honors when we return to Town."

"Thank God for sensible decisions," Jasper exclaimed loudly.

"Amity is the only one in the family I trust not to attempt matchmaking me with one of her more ambitious friends," the duke murmured.

"On that, I think you are correct," Crawford drawled. "Unless you want her help with that as well."

"No." Algernon scowled and turned away. "Come along, little brothers, and Crawford, too. There's much to be done and endured."

He hurried to follow after the duke. "That's right. You're having a meeting with Aston today, aren't you?"

"Yes, unfortunately," the duke said with a heavy sigh. "We returned late enough yesterday that I could put him off without seeming rude, but he will be waiting when we return."

Stratford worried about the outcome of the interview. There was not enough money to repay the man in full. He would not be happy about that and might say so out loud. With George and Edwin seemingly the best of friends, everyone at the palace could hear about the estate's financial problems soon after. Aware that Crawford was near, and left out of the secret, he lowered his voice. "What will you do?"

"I haven't the faintest idea. I had hoped to speak with his son, but with George whispering in his ear all morning, I thought better of making the attempt."

"I never would have imagined that pair striking up a friendship," Stratford said.

"Why wouldn't they be the best of friends? They are mirror images of each other. Ambitious. Gluttonous. Bloodthirsty, when not drinking to excess."

Stratford shook his head. "Edwin Aston used to be so different."

"How so?"

"I don't know," Stratford said, shrugging. "He's certainly not the little fellow I once knew."

Algernon turned to him, a frown on his face. "Explain."

"When I was younger, Father took me with him on a visit to Aston's estate. I got to know Edwin a bit then, although Edwin now claims no memory of the occasion."

"You must have had a gag in your mouth for your whole visit if he doesn't recall how often you would have chattered on," Jasper teased, interrupting. "Lord, all those nights you went on about one thing or another when we were boys, preventing us all from getting any sleep at all."

Stratford thumped his brother's arm. "I don't talk that much."

"Not now, but as a child, the questions and opinions spilling out of your mouth never seemed to end," Algernon added with a slight smile.

Stratford bristled a little. "I like talking."

"We all know that," Nash promised, although it did not sound as much of a complaint from him as usual.

"So, what bothers you about Edwin Aston? That he doesn't remember the visit or your conversations? I suppose it is possible to forget such a momentous event as meeting you, and the slightly less important visit by the Duke of Ravenswood. I'm sure Aston has had many such important visitors over the years, too. He's always curried favor among the aristocracy."

"All of it is wrong." Stratford scratched his head. "It's not the only oddity about him. He… feels different."

"Feels?"

"When we talk, I get a nagging sense he's not the same person I knew," he complained.

"People change as they age."

"Yes, I suppose that could be the cause." He squinted into the distance but there was no longer any sign of Edwin. He'd finally slouched off with George and could already be drinking in the saloon. "He used to run everywhere."

"I highly doubt young Edwin Aston has run a day in life, given his ever-expanding girth," Algernon said with a laugh, clearly amused.

"No. No. He really did run everywhere. I could hardly keep up with him."

"He has changed a great deal then since you first knew him," Algernon suggested gently. "People do."

"His face is also a different shape," Stratford said, puzzled the most about that. If Aston did not claim the man was his son, Stratford would never think them related. Edwin was not the boy he'd played with once. "Wider. And he was smarter than me."

"That's not that hard," Jasper teased.

"Stratford, I'm beginning to really doubt your memory," Algernon complained as the palace loomed closer. "Edwin is ignorant and as boastful as our cousin. If we had a sister, he's the last man I'd ever want to court her. In fact, I would actually forbid any association with him if not for the senior Aston's debt to be paid."

"I could prove it," he said slowly, a thought occurring to him. "I painted Edwin."

"When?"

"When I was younger. Crawford reminded me. After the visit with Father, I was inspired to try to paint portraits and chose him as my first subject."

"So, Edwin is to blame for the countless hours we spent immobile while you painted us,"

Algernon complained, tossing a smile in Stratford's direction.

"It couldn't have been too bad if you asked me to paint you again," Stratford noted sourly.

"Well, I didn't mind because I could read while you did it," Nash offered. "Jasper, though, had to be bribed to remain still for more than five minutes. No patience at all."

All his brothers had complained about sitting for their own portraits. Sometimes he could paint people fairly well from memory, but having a living, breathing body in front of him was always better.

He thought he had done well in Edwin's absence. He'd been rather proud of his efforts, and had more or less given up on landscapes in favor of people from that moment on.

"Do you still have it? The painting of Edwin Aston as a boy?"

Stratford shrugged. "I might. I haven't seen it for a while, actually. It's probably up in the attic with the others if it's anywhere."

"Bring it to me. Perhaps it can have a use as a peace offering with the elder Aston," Ravenswood suggested. "Today will be a difficult day. Find that painting. When we get a look at it, Nash and I will decide if it could be enough to turn the negotiations with Aston in our favor. I fully intend to repay him, but I'd prefer not to beggar us all at once."

Stratford groaned even as he accepted his new

mission to search the attics. He'd hoped to return to his chambers and, if Winston was there, kiss her soundly again.

There was something intoxicating about conducting a secret affair with a woman dressing as a male servant. He was starting to think she might just be worth creating a scandal with, too. He'd never actually had so much fun rolling around, tussling with a woman. She was unique in the way she made him feel. Protective and mischievous. And he wanted to talk to her even more when she suggested he shut his mouth and kiss her.

But talking was his favorite thing to do, and it delayed them reaching the peak of pleasure too soon. Frustrating his fake valet had also become a newfound delight.

He excused himself from his brothers as soon as they were close to the palace and headed directly up to the attics, eager to find the painting so he could return to Win.

The attics were usually a gloomy place at any time of day or night, and he shivered in the musty, cold atmosphere. The deeper he went, the more he detected the faint scent of oil paint in the air.

His old paintings were all neatly arranged against one wall with sheets thrown over each stack, to protect them from the encroaching dust and any light that might fade them. He removed the dust covers one by one as he looked for the oldest stack of completed paintings, hoping the one he sought was among them. If memory served, at the time he was painting this portrait, he had been using smaller square canvases rather than the wider landscapes he'd favored until then.

He flicked through the piles, hoping each one would be the right one.

Finally, nearly last, he found the painting he'd been looking for right at the very back.

He lifted out the square canvas and took it to a shuttered window where the light was better to see it by. It was not his best work, but he felt it was true. A reminder of the boy who he'd tried to befriend long ago.

But it bore no resemblance to Edwin Aston as he appeared now.

He squinted at it in the poor light again and then shook his head. No resemblance whatsoever to the Edwin Aston he'd watched drinking just that morning with Cousin George. The Edwin downstairs towered over his own father, but that was not unusual between generations.

However, even more interesting was that the Edwin Aston he'd once known had been sharp of feature, small for his age, and blond.

The Edwin in the painting had possessed tight blond ringlet curls, too, much like Aston Senior's, though his were grayer now than what they must have been in the man's youth. Stratford had forgotten that important detail about the Edwin he'd known.

He opened the shutters for better illumination and held the painting out at arm's length.

What struck him most was the face. Small, pert nose, almond-shaped eyes, and obvious intelligence shining out from the canvas. When not rushing off, Edwin had always had his head in a book and had not liked Stratford disturbing his reading.

No one ever did, really.

But he would wager the Edwin Aston downstairs probably hadn't lifted a book in years.

The fellow he'd painted had been almost delicate. In fact, if he did not know better, he could almost believe he'd met and painted a daughter of Aston's, rather than the son he remembered being introduced to.

Given the dissimilarity between the painting and Edwin, Aston's heir, it strongly suggested to him that the boy he'd known had been replaced some time ago.

Algernon would certainly want to know about this development. He could perhaps use the information to blackmail Aston into waiting more patiently for a full repayment. It would be a duke's word over Aston's, of course, but it could be enough to simply plant a suspicion and watch the scandal play out.

If it was at all true, that Edwin was an imposter, Aston would fall into line quickly.

If it was not true, well, obviously he would never forgive the duke for casting aspersions on his character. He wasn't disposed to like Algernon anyway, thanks to their father.

But what the hell had happened to the version of Edwin that Stratford had known? Was he dead?

The very thought of that angered him.

Stratford ground his teeth and studied the painting again…

And realized he had seen that slight figure, that sharp jaw and those remarkable eyes—lying under him. The shade of those eyes was something he could never decide upon, even now.

They were as changeable as the weather.

A match for his current valet's.

Stratford cursed. He stared into those eyes and shook his head at another example of his foolishness. Win should be no son of Edwin Aston, but clearly she was something to him. He gulped. Or was it that Edwin Aston the younger was the real stranger in all of this?

He tucked the painting under his arm and turned on his heel.

The Edwin Aston downstairs was a man, once a child, who had been plucked from parts unknown to replace a good son…who might have been a daughter in disguise all along.

Stratford held back a vile curse as he recalled every detail Winston had related about her early life. Always dressed as a boy. Couldn't ever return home. Moving constantly from place to place for employment. Stratford should have asked why she'd ever thought she needed to keep a distance from everyone.

Stratford very much wanted to doubt his conclusions, but they could not be silenced now. Something had bothered him about the younger Edwin Aston for years. Now he knew what it was. Edwin Aston wasn't Edwin Aston.

The Edwin Aston he had known so long ago had been Win.

Win. Edwin.

He thought of the name she used, and cursed again.

Edwin Aston even spelled Dane Winston if you scrambled the letters around and added Edwin's middle initial. N.

It was a game Stratford played in his head when he was bored. He'd taught Edwin how to do it, and they had played it together as children, at night when Stratford couldn't fall asleep and had kept Edwin from slumber, too. He closed his eyes, remembering the almost forgotten occasion. Edwin lying in his bed beside Stratford's in the nursery, pulling his blankets up to his chin, and getting cranky with Stratford for talking too much.

Rotted Fretsaws.

That was the unfortunate name Edwin had made up for Stratford one night. Odd how he had not forgotten after all these years. Edwin had repeated it over and over and over to him, and said nothing else. Stratford hadn't been able to get him to stop until he'd promised to shut up.

He put the painting up to the light again as he passed another window. He'd bet his future profits from the Ravenswood estate that this portrait was of his current lover as a child. Likely the only proof of her existence.

Which begged the question: why?

Why was she here now? Was it only chance that had brought them together?

And what would Aston do when he saw Win again, if she was his long-lost daughter?

He gulped at the thought of that scandal engulfing them all.

Was her father's anger the reason Winston had said she could never go home? Was she afraid of the man she resembled more than a little, now that Stratford considered their features? The similarity was definitely there. But to be sure, he'd need to see them together in the same room, at the same time.

He scolded himself roundly. He should have seen it before. He studied people for fun and had missed all the signs of a familiar face and old friend in hers. The servant he'd plucked from a shabby inn and promoted to be his valet on a whim had been no whim at all. No wonder he'd agreed so readily to taking Win on. He'd felt an instant connection.

But Win? She should have run the other way if she'd recognized him. Win likely had no idea who he'd been to her, or she would never have wanted to be anywhere near him again. He'd been really annoying as a child. But he couldn't help but smile now.

He'd found his friend of old at that inn, and his soul had known not to let him, or rather her, slip through his fingers a second time.

Chapter Fourteen

F ate and Stratford conspired to prevent Winston from reaching an exit to Ravenswood until it was much too late to leave unnoticed. She had wanted to be on her way hours ago, but unfortunately had fallen back asleep after he had gone shooting. She had woken an hour later than she ought and now was in something of a rush. "You're late," she warned herself, even as she threw herself out of his bed.

There really had been no opportunity for any goodbye.

The worry was whether her father was awake already, and what he might do when and if he ever saw her face again.

Her joy in the night and the morning she'd shared with Stratford, as he'd whispered scandalous things about what they were doing to each other as they made love, was fading now that he was gone. But fade it must, and she was determined—she could not stay a moment longer and let her father catch sight of her.

Winston remade the bed neatly, and then mussed it up as if only one person had spent the night alone in it. All evidence of their passion, of her gender, had to be hidden from the gossiping maids who would come to the room soon.

Once satisfied all was as it should be in the bedchamber, Winston headed into the dressing closet again to collect her possessions for her journey.

When she emerged from the room, she felt a twinge of guilt for abandoning her post. But she had no time for foolish sentimentality. Her father should be rising anytime soon.

She hurried down the servant stair, satchel slung over one shoulder. Thankfully, the servants who slept up in the attics seemed not to be moving about yet. That wasn't to say there couldn't be someone in the kitchen, stoking a fire to boil water for tea.

She cautiously set one foot in the servants' hall and looked around quickly to determine if anyone might already be awake. The halls were still dark, but it would not be long before the entire house woke and started the endless task of providing for a house full of hungry guests.

Relieved not to see anyone, she was about to turn away when a woman cried out in pain. Startled, she narrowed her eyes on the larder, where she noted the door was ajar. It should have been locked if Cook wasn't around, which meant Cook was already awake, and she'd hurt herself.

Winston set her satchel down on a chair out of the way and hurried toward that open doorway.

But a man's figure stood just inside the door, with his back to her.

"That wasn't nice," he complained

Winston recognized the voice. Philips—the fellow who had most likely locked her out of the manor on her first night here. He was currently blocking the doorway and, if she was not mistaken, he was not alone in there.

She moved closer and caught a glimpse of the cook, with cheeks flushed pink with anger. Mrs. Derry had pressed herself against the far wall as Philips crowded her.

Winston moved to one side of the door to listen to the exchange inside before deciding if she would be interrupting an assignation or an imposition. Affairs between servants were generally frowned upon.

"Why so cold, pet?"

"You tricked me, you blackguard," Mrs. Derry accused.

"You wanted it, too," Philips promised in a tone that turned Winston's stomach. "There's no reason for false modesty now."

"Get out before the butler arrives," she hissed.

"Imagine the old fool's shock seeing you like this with me. He thinks you a chaste and proper matron. When he finds out you've been sneaking into the larder to meet me, he will be so disappointed in you."

"You seduced me. You've as much to lose as I do."

"Seymour doesn't control my fate the way he does yours. Besides, I was seduced into an assignation with an older woman."

"That's not true."

"You knew I couldn't resist the temptation of a private sampling of your best preserves," Philips suggested with a course laugh. "I won't resist tomorrow, either. I'll be waiting again when everyone's still abed."

"You'll wait a long time for anything from me again," Mrs. Derry warned. "Not without the banns being called."

The man merely laughed.

Winston had heard enough to know Mrs. Derry was in an impossible position and bound for disappointment from someone like Philips. Winston glanced around. She couldn't shout out the woman's name, but a noise of some sort in the kitchen could separate them.

There was a copper roasting pan on a nearby work surface and Winston sent it sailing across the room to land under a far chair, out of harm's way, and then hid herself.

"Let me pass. Someone's out there!" Mrs. Derry whispered in a panicked voice as she emerged from the larder alone. "Who's there?" she called, smoothing down her apron.

After a moment of hearing nothing in reply, Philips emerged, smirking, and skulked off quickly down the hallway and disappeared without another word.

Once assured he was gone, Winston emerged from hiding and cleared her throat.

Mrs. Derry gasped to see Winston standing so close. "What can I do for you, sir?"

"Nothing, Mrs. Derry. But is there something I can do for you?" Winston tipped her head toward the larder doorway rather than voice her concern out loud.

Mrs. Derry gasped again and took a step back, misunderstanding her concern as likely something highly improper.

Winston shook her head. "How long has that scoundrel been seeking you out?"

The woman looked puzzled. "What man?"

"Philips. He imposed upon you," Winston suggested gently. It wasn't easy to be a woman in a male-dominated society. That was why she didn't try. Male servants definitely had the upper hand in the servant realm. Philips should be made to own up to his lecherous actions and marry her though.

"I don't know to what you are inferring but I won't have it in my presence," she said, bristling with indignation.

Winston admired her for a moment, but it was clear the woman was disturbed by the encounter she'd just had with Philips in the larder. She did not have the look of a woman in love, either. Winston lowered her voice. "You should tell someone that he's bothering you."

"I don't know what you're talking about," Mrs.

Derry assured her, but she looked worried. She probably thought Winston would tell on her.

"Or at least speak with the housekeeper about it. She could help you avoid further incidents like that," Winston murmured, jerking her thumb toward the larder.

The cook's eyes narrowed. "You should return to your duties and cease meddling in the affairs of the kitchen," she snapped.

Winston understood only too well that the woman feared exposure for carrying on any sort of relationship with a fellow servant. Even if she had wanted the attentions of the footman Philips initially, she would be the one to suffer for it eventually if he'd no honorable intentions toward her. At best she'd suffer a marriage, but most likely she'd be cast out of a position of long-held trust. Philips wasn't a member of staff here, and in Winston's opinion, he didn't seem the type to want to marry, especially an older lady like Mrs. Derry.

Winston retreated, for now, but vowed to keep an eye on Philips whenever she could.

She pulled a face and looked up at the ceiling briefly to curse the sense of honor that had been drilled into her from birth. She'd made a promise to her father as a boy to protect those weaker than her from mistreatment. The cook needed her help whether she wanted it or not.

Winston headed into the servants' staircase, satchel slung over her shoulder again, and returned to her employer's chambers, only to find Lord Stratford in the room already, sitting in the armchair facing the door.

He looked up when he saw her, and she smiled until she remembered her satchel was still hanging over her shoulder. She set it down quickly behind a chair, hoping he hadn't noticed. "Lord Stratford," she murmured, walking toward him.

He glanced down at the satchel. "Explain why you have that?"

"Cuthbert will return soon," she explained. "I wanted to be ready."

"You were not ready two days ago," he said, eyes narrowing on her face. "In fact, I had the distinct impression you might never want to leave my side, given recent events."

"You did not offer me a permanent position."

"I offered me, and I don't offer that to just any lady."

"In London, not here," she reminded him.

"Anywhere and everywhere," he promised. He drew in a deep breath and stood slowly. He took his time reaching her, and when he did, he only looked down into her face with his lips pursed. "I want to show you something," he said finally.

"Of course, my lord."

The frown on his face grew more pronounced as he stared at her. "Is there something you want to tell me?"

"No."

His eyes narrowed. "Has something happened?"

"No, my lord."

He wet his lips. "Does anyone but me know about you yet?"

"No, of course not," she assured quickly. "My gender is no one's business but my own."

"I thought the same once."

Winston smiled at him, despite the odd questions. She pushed at his arm, hoping to snap him out of whatever thoughts were in his head. "What was it you wanted to show me?"

Lord Stratford strode away to the bed and pulled a canvas out from under it. He held it out before him and then put it on his easel. "Come and look at this, Win."

Winston dutifully went to stand beside her employer to look at what she assumed must be one of his paintings. It was definitely his work. A painting of a young boy...

A sweat broke out over Winston's entire body as she recognized the face.

It was a painting of her as a child.

She did not remember sitting for this painting or having made the acquaintance of Stratford before meeting him at the inn. But she must have known him. Once. That would explain her intense reaction to him at their first meeting. Winston made herself nod in admiration of the likeness, but her mind was in a whirl. How had she been so stupid not to recall meeting her employer before?

She swallowed the lump in her throat. "Is it one of your brothers?"

"None of us had hair so pale or curly." He looked down on her, and then he moved to stand behind her and held her in his arms. "Do you see this fellow's eyes? What shade do you think they are?"

She pretended to squint at the painting, heart in her throat the entire time. It was a good likeness of her. "I don't truly know, my lord."

Lord Stratford's arms tightened around her. "I never did either. They are like yours. As changeable as the weather."

She gulped and tried not to squirm. "Was this boy a friend of yours?"

"No. He was my enemy for some reason."

"Your enemy?"

Stratford released her and moved to stand beside the painting he'd done. "The fellow took an instant dislike to me. I tried everything possible to win his good graces, too, fool that I was back then. Some things never change really."

Winston suddenly remembered meeting Lord Stratford Sweet, and blanched. An important visitor had come to her father's estate, and he had brought a young boy with him one summer. Winston had entirely forgotten the family name until this moment, but it must have been the late Duke of Ravenswood and his youngest son.

The man standing before her now had dogged her steps for the whole of his visit, talking nonstop. Winston had never had a friend before and had enjoyed being around someone her own age at first. But then Mother had warned her not to become comfortable around the young lad. Stratford had been inquisitive even then, and he still was, it seemed. It had been hard to rebuff Stratford when she was a child, and now she'd failed again. She was in trouble indeed. She had come full circle.

"I'm sure it was nothing you did," she said carefully, turning away, determined not to give herself up. There was still a slim chance she could explain away the resemblance through denial or coincidence.

"Oh, I'm sure I was an annoying insect back then. Quite crushed by the snub for a long time." He remained near the painting, but she could feel his eyes upon her. "I didn't see him again for the longest time. When we met again, years later, he even denied the time we'd spent together as boys. I painted this from memory of him, after I returned home from my visit. I could never exactly capture the essence of the fellow or perhaps understand my frustration and fascination with him then."

Winston was unexpectedly touched by the gesture. She'd always hated sitting still for portraits. She'd been utterly horrible to Stratford by the end of his visit, too. She'd expected, hoped, to have been forgotten over the intervening years by everyone. But knowing she had made such an impression on that chattering young boy changed nothing. She was not that young lad he'd painted. She never had been.

Winston forced a smile. "It was good of you to keep such a charming memento of him."

She bent to pick up a discarded coat of his and rushed to find a brush to remove the nearly imperceptible grass on the sleeve. She hoped that could be the end of the discussion as she walked away, but of course, Lord Stratford would want the last word as usual.

"Fortunate, too," he called, turning the easel until it faced them both.

Winston ignored the painting, unsettled by looking at herself, and brushed the coat all over again. "Why fortunate?"

"Well, surely you can see the resemblance as clearly as I can?"

"Resemblance?"

"There is an Edwin staying as a guest at the estate, and I have to say the boy I painted looks nothing like him now."

She made herself shrug but hearing that her father's other son was also called Edwin startled her. "People change."

"Yes, my brother the duke said much the same when I mentioned my suspicions." He tilted his head to one side as he peered at her face. "Yes, indeed. Suspicions that cannot be silenced now, I'm afraid."

She gulped and rushed into the closet to hang the coat on a peg. Once beyond Lord Stratford's sight, she closed her eyes and let out a shaky breath. She was found out entirely now. If Stratford could see a similarity, then there was no hiding from her father. If he caught a glimpse of her face, he'd know her in an instant, and she really would have to run away as fast as her legs could carry her.

"I could almost believe you brother and sister," he whispered.

She turned to find Stratford had followed her into the closet. "You have quite the imagination, my lord."

"I said almost," he said, grabbing her chin gently and turned her gaze to face the damning portrait he held.

Chapter Fifteen

Stratford did not believe Win's protests. She was Mr. Aston's daughter. No matter what she said to the contrary, the similarity was as clear as day to him now.

She had once been Edwin Aston. She had invented a family that suited the story she peddled to others, but it did not sound reasonable now, given the other things she'd said about her life.

"Win, there is no point in lying anymore," he whispered. "I know who you are and that you were cast out. My only question is why?"

"I'm no relation of Aston's," she said quickly.

Too quickly.

He drew closer and smiled down at her pale face, determined to get her to admit to the truth. "For the record...I never said my friend's name was Aston."

Win swallowed and cast her eyes downward. "I thought you said he was your enemy."

"I wanted to be his friend then. I am yours now. I can help you settle the score with your father. Make him own up to his deception."

Her gaze shot to his. "What deception would that be?"

"Come now, Win. I know it all now. Aston

parades a fellow about, claiming the man to be his son, Edwin. But that man is not the Edwin I met as a boy. Aston lies to the world. The other boy is likely a bastard or an orphan snatched from the gutter. He's living a better life playing a rich man's son when those riches should have gone to his daughter's dowry."

Win stumbled back from him. "What good would revealing this charade you imagine he's perpetuating do anyone?"

"It would help you and your mother, I'm sure," he promised, recalling how the woman had been at odds with her husband for years.

"She's dead," Win assured him with more than a trace of bitterness in her tone.

"No, Win," he promised, attempting to take hold of her hands. "I assure you, Mrs. Aston is alive and well, or was last season when I saw her in Town."

Win staggered back a few more steps, eyes wide on his, her face pale. "That cannot be. She drowned."

"Come again?"

"My mother drowned in the accident."

"What accident, Win?"

Win turned away suddenly and walked to the windows, hand over her mouth. "No. You are mistaken."

"Come now, Win. You look too much like my old friend to be a mere coincidence. You are Aston's child, and I will tell everyone who matters in these things that he should be made to support you."

"Don't do that!" Winston snapped. "I want nothing I haven't earned from my own labors."

"He's a rich man," Stratford murmured. "Not without influence in certain circles. You could do far better in life than you ever dare imagine with his financial support. My brother can make him do the right thing. We can confront him together." He drew close to her again and put his fingers lightly on her shoulder. "But Win, what accident were you talking about?"

Win turned on him then, eyes wild, breathing rushed.

"I've never heard of Mrs. Aston being involved in any accident," he said gently.

She wet her lips and turned her head to stare at the door to his room. "Is she here? Mrs. Aston."

"No. Your parents quarrel bitterly, and they live separate lives. Even her false son wants nothing to do with her, I've heard."

Winston started to nod but then rushed away from him, snatched up the chamber pot and cast up her accounts into it. Stratford winced, following to offer his assistance, but she pushed him away and propped herself up against a doorway, face pale and sweaty and visibly shaken by all he'd told her.

Slowly she slid down the wall. When she hugged her knees and laid her head down on them, Stratford took the opportunity to take the chamber pot from her, open a window, and throw the contents outside. He left the windows wide open to let in some fresh air and then sat himself down cross-legged opposite her and waited.

Win finally looked up at him. It was clear she was devastated. Her defenses lowered. The fight gone from her.

He winced. "You thought she was dead."

Win nodded quickly.

"Tell me what happened. You were in a boat?"

"No," she promised, wiping her face with the back of her hand. "Mama bundled me into a carriage late one night. I don't remember where we were supposed to be going. We were speeding away from Father, he was angry...and then we were in the river. I heard her scream for help and then she stopped. I assumed she was lost, pulled under by the weight of her skirts. But she's alive— and I should be dead."

Stratford inched closer. "Don't you want to stop running? Wouldn't you like to see your mama again?"

She looked up at him, eyes huge. "No. I never want to see her again."

Stratford was taken aback by the venom in her words. She sounded like she hated her mother. Had her mother betrayed her too? He reached for her hand and attempted to clasp it in his. "My mistake."

"Yes." She laid her head back against the wall

and closed her eyes. "One of many, I'm afraid, my lord."

"Then correct me where I'm wrong. It is you," he whispered. "The boy who hated me."

"You always were a persistent devil," she complained. "Forever nagging me to play your games."

He grinned then, so utterly relieved to know he was right about her. "Games are fun, and you could learn a lot from me."

Win sat up straighter and met his gaze. "And you wonder why we never got along as children. You always have to have the last word."

"It annoys my brothers, too." He nodded quickly. "Tell me how this happened to you."

"How what happened?"

"How you came to this point in your life. Go back to when we met and tell me everything that happened after," he suggested. When her lips pursed tightly, he added, "You can trust me."

"No one who says that is trustworthy," she replied, a tight smile on her lips.

"Then look in your heart, Win. Am I worthy of your friendship?"

Her smile grew strained. "It's impossible but…"

"But you want to believe in me. I know you do." Stratford wriggled forward until they sat just touching at the knees. "I want to believe in you too. You are my oldest friend."

"We were never friends," she reminded him.

"I'm not so bad. In fact, I think there are distinct advantages to our renewed acquaintance," he promised.

"Such as?"

He spread his hands wide. "I am the easiest of men and extremely loyal."

"Like a lap dog?"

"How about you sit on mine," he suggested with a laugh that brought a blush to her cheeks. "I'm much too big for that tiny little lap of yours. I'd probably squash you."

"Size isn't all that matters," she promised.

"To real men it is," he promised with a wink. He inhaled deeply and brought her cold hand to his lips to kiss. "We have years of catching up to do, Win. Let's start with how you came to be alone after we met."

"My story begins earlier than that. I have to go back to the time before I was born," she whispered and sighed. "My mother was desperate to give her husband the son he demanded she bear him."

"I've never heard him speak of your mother with any kindness," he confessed, and then he pointed to the portrait still sitting upon the easel. "I had intended to give him that painting. But I wonder if I should make the attempt now."

"Why would you want to give him a present of my likeness after all this time?"

"Hmm," Stratford said, and then cleared his throat. "Since we're trading secrets, I suppose I must trust you with some truth, too. There's been

210 | HEATHER BOYD

a bit of awkwardness since my father died and my brother took over the estate. Something we're trying to hush up. My late father apparently owed yours a great deal of money, and now the repayment has become my brother's cross to bear. Your father likely came here to collect the amount in full. I thought giving him that portrait might soften his heart a little."

"I would say it would do the opposite," she warned.

"Hmm, that is the conclusion I am fast reaching myself. Unfortunately, I had already mentioned the painting to my brothers before learning who you really were. They still intend to give it to him in the hopes he will not demand immediate repayment of those debts."

"Oh," she whispered, turning to look at it again. "Even then that boy had secrets. Especially from you."

"I assume your mother was complicit in the decision to hide your gender, which is why your parents live separate lives now. She must have been destroyed to lose you."

"It was my life that was destroyed. It was Mama's decision entirely to pass me off as my father's son," she whispered. "Giving Father a reminder of my existence would not help with the debt. It will anger him. Mother had cruelly deceived him for years, after all. So had I, and he became enraged when he discovered the truth. Mama tried to flee with me, and then the accident happened. There is no telling what he might do or say if he knew I was still alive, but it would not soften his heart one little bit—if he has one anymore. You can't let him know about me."

"I won't if you don't want me to." Stratford shifted to her side and put his arm about her shoulders. The first time he'd ever done so. It felt...nice. She felt nicer to him by the moment. Even with her surly bossiness and habit of wearing trousers. He could now understand why she lived the way she did. "We will think of something else to manage the debt," Stratford promised, and then glanced over to the painting. "It's not my best work but I think I captured the essence of you."

Win leaned her head against his shoulder. "When did you paint it?"

"After I came home from our visit. I was frustrated and...and I got lost remembering the expression on your face the last time I saw you."

She laughed softly. "I remember. I must be honest. I had been relieved to see the back of you that day. It had grown increasingly difficult being around you. You asked so many questions, determined to know everything about me and my life. In any other circumstances, had I been anyone else, I might have been flattered. But I'd known the trouble you could have caused me if I let down my guard." She shook her head. "I always thought my father murdered my mother for her deception."

"Why did you think it murder?"

"He knew about me." Win shook her head. "Mama said he was chasing after us. Urged the coachman to whip the horses to a faster pace to outrun him. But the carriage rocked so badly that it sent us right off a bridge. Father was there on the bank."

Stratford's eyes widened. "How did you not drown?"

"I could swim and only had to kick off my shoes and let the current take me wherever it cared to. I knew I couldn't go back to him and expect kindness. He wanted me gone. Erased along with the lie of my life. But he didn't end my life. He gave it to someone else."

Stratford pulled her close and kissed her head, wishing he might settle the score with Aston over his treatment of Win. "You must have been terrified. Being all alone in the dark."

She shrugged away his sympathy. "No worse than living a lie and expecting discovery at any moment."

He expelled a heavy breath. "You'll be safer with me. I want to help. I am your friend."

She looked up at him. "You understand why I couldn't be before, when we were younger."

"Oh, yes, but that doesn't matter now," he nodded and released her to get to his feet.

Win caught his fingers, and he helped her up from the floor. "I should have recognized you. You haven't changed at all."

Stratford grinned. "Do you remember that day

we escaped together? Snuck out in the early morning before even the servants rose and ran as far and as fast as we could?"

"Actually, I had been trying to sneak away from you before you woke up that morning. You teased me about being too slow to dodge you."

"And you were too haughty to even come swimming with me," he complained. "Wouldn't even get your feet wet."

"If I had removed my clothes, you would have immediately detected the difference between us and told everyone."

Stratford threw a slightly embarrassed smile her way and then shrugged. "Well, obviously it makes more sense now that I know you were female, but I refuse to believe I would have tattled." Win's life had been one endless nightmare, but a new day was dawning for them both. "It's good to talk to you again, Edwin."

She gulped. "It's has been good, Rotted Fretsaws."

"Oh, you had to remember that!" he complained and then hugged her tightly when she laughed. "You must stay with me. I don't want him finding you alone on the long drive or on the road to the nearest town. I can protect you from him. There's no reason to fear him anymore."

Winston looked up at him with huge eyes that slowly softened. "All right, I'll stay, but only as your valet until Cuthbert comes."

"You still argue like that boy. I could never

convince you to do anything." He grinned then. "Hide this in the closet. I'll be back before you know it."

"Where are you going?"

"I have to tell my brothers the painting is lost."

He gave Win a quick kiss of farewell and headed for the door.

As he walked down the hall, he realized he liked Win, much more than he'd ever liked anyone else. She challenged him in ways he hadn't been ready for in the beginning. But he'd recovered from all those shocks to the point where he looked forward to what might happen next. She was bossy, but he enjoyed frustrating her. And Win could not hope to avoid discovery forever. One day, she might have to consider packing away her breeches, and when she did, he'd be there to support her decision.

He made his way downstairs and along to the duke's study.

He quietly slipped into the room and closed the door behind him before looking around. All the family, the ones who mattered, were gathered together around the duke's desk again. The ledgers open wide.

Crawford was there too, bent over them, studying the figures.

He slowed his steps, surprised to see him. "What's to do?"

"I took your advice and invited Crawford to join us today."

"The second invitation from you I would rather not have accepted," he murmured quietly.

"At least now your bride will understand our long faces are for a good reason," the duke answered.

Amity Crawford was perched by the fire. "I do apologize if my curiosity has caused additional concern."

"It is of no matter now, cousin," Algernon promised. "You would have learned of the problem before the season started and you became my hostess in London."

"Yes, that is information I would have needed," she said, smiling quickly at the duke. "I shall have to be even more discerning when deciding upon my guest lists than I initially expected to be."

"I'd appreciate that," Algernon replied. "Now, since everyone is here. Aston has made it quite clear he requires an immediate payment of all outstanding debts."

They all swore.

"But Stratford was telling me earlier today about a painting he did of Edwin Aston as a boy. I mentioned it to Aston, and he showed great interest in seeing it. I was thinking of gifting it to him anyway, with Stratford's permission, of course." Algernon's gaze flickered in Stratford's direction. "Have you found it?"

Put on the spot, Stratford shuffled his feet. "Unfortunately not. Are you sure giving him the painting will help?"

"Yes, but do you now think it won't?"

"I don't think it will," Jasper announced. "Has anyone but me noticed that the Astons never look directly at each other? I think there is bad blood between father and son."

"It never used to be that way," Stratford murmured.

He had once felt a little jealous of the older Aston's smile for his only offspring. Stratford's own father had never looked at him the same way. Only his brothers had ever made him feel he belonged.

"I should like to see this painting you did, Stratford," Amity announced. "It could certainly help soften Aston if it is well done."

Crawford leaned toward his wife and patted her hand. "Stratford only painted the portrait from his memory, my love."

"A memory he fears may not have been accurate, too, I should caution," Algernon murmured to everyone.

"It was a long time ago and people change," Stratford muttered.

"You've always been your harshest critic, brother," Nash complained. "I am certain it will be as accurate a portrait as any you've ever done."

Stratford blushed. It was an accurate portrait indeed. Win had not changed that much since being Edwin Aston. "I will have another look for it."

"Good, I want Aston to leave knowing we went out of the way to honor his family and that the connection means something to us still. We have a long way to go before he approves of us. Father did an excellent job of painting his sons in the harshest light possible."

"I'm certain George did his part, too, over the years," Amity murmured. "If there was a close bond between Edwin Aston and his father once, I'm certain the painting might foster a return of affection between them one day soon."

Given what he knew now, Stratford doubted it. If that painting came to light, if it were placed beside the imposter heir, others might begin to doubt the fellow's identity too.

"We need to see that painting, brother," Algernon said, giving Stratford a long hard look. "Go and have another look for it."

Dismissed, he returned slowly upstairs and went to the attics again to make it seem like he was looking around for the old painting, pretending he didn't already have it hidden in his chambers. He left the stacks uncovered and untidy to show he'd been up there, should anyone else come looking too.

Then he returned to his chamber in the hope of finding Winston still there.

She was polishing his evening slippers to a

high shine. She looked startled to see him and stood. "What did they say?"

"They still want it, Win," he replied sourly.

"Oh," she murmured, and then nodded.

"But I won't give it up, or you, either," he said as he went to her and brushed his finger along her jaw. They were becoming something more than he'd ever imagined they might be. He wanted more such moments where they talked about their lives. What they wanted and where they might go next together. But first he had to deal with the painting. He would not destroy it, but he stashed it in his dressing closet far at the back.

When he returned to his bedchamber where Win was polishing his riding boots, the rhythmic swing and swoop of her movements were mesmerizing. He shook his head and stilled her hands to regain her attention. "Be cautious on your travels through the house."

"I always am," she promised without looking up.

Stratford leaned down and dropped a kiss on her head. "I wish things could be different."

"You know they cannot."

He turned away, frustrated. He'd never had this before. Companionship and friendship and a woman he desired no matter what she wore. He'd never had to hide his feelings for a woman in his life.

He headed to the easel, a place where he often

found answers to the questions he'd not even asked himself yet.

The unfinished painting was still there, and glaringly bad. He had come to loathe the work and, after a moment's consideration, set it aside.

He picked up a blank fresh canvas, and as he looked across the room to where Win toiled over his boots, inspiration struck. What he wanted was this, to capture this moment and hold it forever in his memory. But he had no idea if Win could ever want the same.

Just the two of them…perhaps falling in love.

Chapter Sixteen

Although it was an hour until sunrise, Winston crept from Lord Stratford's chamber and into the hall. Since she was staying, she meant to make good on her vow to protect the cook from Philips' unwanted advances. Or if she was too late, make sure the scoundrel was found out so he would make an honest woman of her.

The occupants of this part of the house, guests, were hours away from waking, thankfully, and she expected to see no one at all around. The hallway was cast in deep shadows broken only by the light of the waning moon. She moved swiftly down the hall, keeping her steps light and noiseless, hoping to rouse no one with her passage to the servants' staircase.

She had almost made it when a tired voice rang out, startling herself with its proximity.

"I see I'm not the only one unable to stay asleep," a voice murmured to her right.

Winston froze, recognizing the voice in an instant as belonging to her father. What was he doing awake at this hour?

"No, sir," she mumbled, dipping her chin low so he could not see too much of her face.

Thankfully the darkness would mask most of her features. "Good morning."

"Good it is not, for I have not managed a wink of sleep all night and it has left me with a bitter taste in my mouth."

"I'm sorry, sir. Is there anything I can do?"

Winston kicked herself for making that offer. But it was out of her mouth and could not be taken back.

He drew closer, limping. "You're a servant here?"

"Yes, sir. I'm Lord Stratford's valet."

"Ah, so you work for the younger son of the old duke," he said as he brushed past her shoulders. "I'm sure he will not mind if I appropriate your services for a moment. Come with me."

Winston quaked and turned slowly, keeping her chin down still. "How might I be of service?"

"An object fell from my hand and rolled under the bed earlier in the evening. I am unable to reach it myself," he grumbled. "Get it for me."

"I'd be more than happy to fetch it, sir," she promised, nodding and ducking through his doorway. She crossed the darkened room, relieved there were no candles lit. The bed seemed to be in a terrible shambles from his restless attempts to fall sleep.

She flicked up the bedding hanging over the side and ducked under the frame, easily finding the pencil he'd lost. It was the kind she'd once used for her own lessons with the endless tutors he'd hired for her as a child. She scrambled out again, brushed off her front in case of dust and placed the pencil on a table beside the bed instead of giving it to him directly. She did not want to get too close. She could not allow him to see her face clearly. "If there's nothing else?"

"You might stir the fire and light a few candles. I dislike the dark."

"The dark is only the absence of light," Winston answered. She bent to the task of stirring the fire, trying not to worry about the silence behind her.

When the flames had risen sufficiently, she stood to snatch up a candlestick to light the rest with. Father shuffled to a chair close to the fire and sat himself down with a groan. "Ah, that's better. I should have done it myself but it's much easier and less painful to have someone younger than me do the bending."

Winston lighted the candles placed far away from him and then bowed in his vague direction. "You're welcome, sir."

"Oh, do not leave before you light this one right here by my side. I feel inclined to read a while."

She gulped. To reach that candle, she had to stand directly in front of him. "Yes, sir."

Winston carried a lighted candle across the room to do his bidding. She kept her eyes on the flames—even as she heard her father gasp out loud.

She lit the candle for him. There could be no hiding her face with so much illumination shining upon it now.

She looked down at him. Facing her fear. His expression was one of utter shock to see her standing there.

She inclined her head and asked, "If there's nothing else, sir."

When he seemed incapable of answering, Winston took that as a sign it was time to depart the room. She knew that once he'd thought about her existence a little longer, he could have a great many unpleasant things to say to her. She'd rather not hear any of it.

Winston stalked out of the room and left the door wide open behind her. Went to the servants' stairs and rushed down them. She burst out of the stairwell and threw her back against it and buried her face in her hands.

Father had seen her! He might come after her. Decry her existence and expose her disguise to everyone. He could use her charade as a means of embarrassing Stratford, and the entire Sweet family.

"No," she said—at the same time another woman did, too. And then that other woman kept on saying the word as the sounds of a struggle became clearer.

Win threw herself off the door and searched

for the altercation, finding Philips accosting Mrs. Derry on the kitchen floor.

Mrs. Derry was putting up a good fight, but Philips was far stronger. He would get what he wanted from the woman if someone didn't help her.

Win threw herself bodily into the fray, knocking Philips away from the woman. Win spared Mrs. Derry a brief glance as she scrambled away, hoping she was not too late. She turned back to Philips, noting his trousers were still buttoned. Yes, she'd prevented the worst but now what of tomorrow, or the next day?

"You stay away from Mrs. Derry!"

Philips swung out one arm, intending to knock Winston aside. "Mind your own business."

Win dodged that arm and then grabbed it, turning Philips back to face her. "You leave her alone."

Philips smiled. "She's mine."

"You gutter-born blackguard," Win snarled, gesturing behind her back for Cook to get out of the room while she could. "No woman deserves to be pawed at by you."

Philips curled his hands into fists. "You think you're better than me?"

"Anyone is better than you."

Philips suddenly grabbed Win by the cravat and lifted her up until her feet dangled above the floor. "A baby-faced boy like you wouldn't know how to satisfy a woman."

"Probably not," Win conceded. "But I'm big enough to teach you some manners."

"Hardly." Philips smiled slowly. "You won't win against me, you know."

"Prove it then," she dared. "Outside. Now."

Philips barked a laugh. "It would be my pleasure to rub your nose into the earth and see you choke on it, but I think I'll stay right here. She'll be back."

"You think you can best me," Winston said, thinking quickly. She might not win in the end, but she could also not back down. A lady's honor was at stake. "You think I won't tell everyone what you've done and make sure you marry her."

She wouldn't tattle but he didn't need to know that. Win could not condemn Derry to having this man as a husband. She just had to delay Philips here a bit longer, until someone came along and sent for the butler to put a stop to their argument.

Philips regarded her sourly. "Why you little…"

"Or are you too cowardly to face me," Win taunted. "Can't get a woman into your bed without forcing her there.

"You've a smart mouth for a skinny little fellow," Philip's said, puffing out his chest and clenching his fists. "I'll enjoy wiping the floor with you right here and now."

"We fight outside or be known as a coward, you great lumbering clod. If I win, you will never

ever lay one finger on any woman at the palace," Winston demanded.

"If I win, you leave. If you're able to," he finished. "Outside it is."

Winston followed until they arrived at a lush patch of lawn.

"Are you ready?" she asked, rolling up her sleeves.

But Philips played by ungentlemanly rules and tackled Winston to the ground before she was ready.

"Bad form, sir," Winston chided, wriggling out from under his bulk and bouncing to her feet.

Philips was slower to get up. "Who are you, the king of England?"

"The king lets others fight for him," Winston retorted. "Don't you know anything about the world, you great lumbering brute? Can you even read?"

Insults were customary, and Winston hurled her best at the other valet. If he was angry, he would strike out without thinking clearly, and Winston would make the most of those chances to strike back when he gave her any chance.

"What's going on out there?" someone shouted out from somewhere above their heads.

Win did not dare answer.

She circled Philips, becoming aware that one by one, windows above them were opening to view the fight below. It surely would not be long before someone came to separate them. Winston only had to hold out that long.

Philips swung his fist suddenly and caught Winston a glancing blow on the jaw.

Someone cried out. Win didn't look around to see who it had been as she staggered back, dazed momentarily.

Philips wasn't close enough to hit her again. He looked around, beaming a wide smile. "Excuse me a moment while I teach this young pup a lesson he'll not forget," Philips said, playing up to their audience and getting a cheer in return from some of the guests hanging out the windows on the upper level.

Next came the footmen and maids, bursting out of every doorway, running to surround them, forming a tight circle from which there was no escape.

Winston rushed Philips, who simply tossed her into the crowd.

They threw her back toward the center again.

Philips ignored her for a moment and puffed out his chest. "The new man has decided to start his day by being trounced by his superior valet."

A twitter of laughter swept through the crowd.

"Shall I put him in his place?"

A cheer went up for yes and then bets started being placed on the outcome. None of them in Winston's favor.

She rubbed her jaw, wondering why she'd assumed the fighting would be stopped. Men were bloodthirsty creatures, and greedy for a win at any cost.

She saw Mrs. Derry standing among the crowd. Her face pale but largely composed. Winston turned away from her, knowing there was nothing that could stop the fight now.

She faced off with Philips again, squaring her shoulders.

"Edwin, stop this at once," Father shouted over the din of the bidding servants.

She turned to look at him as he pushed his way to the front, and their eyes met. Unfortunately, Philips took a swing for her head at that exact moment. She saw it coming out the corner of her eye and bent backward to avoid it, flipping onto her hands and again onto her feet at the edge of the circle.

The crowd roared with laughter. Quick as a wink, she was back at Philips, jabbing at his soft unprotected sides, then raising her hands to ward off another blow the way she'd been taught.

Always get back up, Father had said. It was a mark of a man of small stature not to cower.

"I said stop!" Father bellowed. "Have you no dignity for the spectacle you are making of yourself?"

There was no mistaking that warning was meant for Winston. But before she could answer, someone else did.

"Father, it's just a bit of harmless fun between the servants," the replacement Edwin called out from somewhere behind her. "Go back to bed. Or would you care to wager on the little one's chances? I give him one in ten."

Winston clenched her jaw and kept her eye on her large opponent, who was following the exchange.

"This is madness," Father said to everyone. "Stop at once, do you hear."

But the fight wasn't over just because he said so. Her honor was at stake. The pride of the Ravenswood servants, too.

Another man pushed through—someone who looked a lot like Lord Stratford. "What's the meaning of this?"

She spared him a glance and then automatically straightened. This had to be the Duke of Ravenswood.

A footman whispered the particulars of the fight to him, and although he didn't look happy, he stepped back and nodded. "Have Lord Nash sent for then."

Given that his words stirred the servants to hoot with joy, she assumed the fight could continue under his gaze. But with the duke presiding over them, there might be some adherence of the rules, but she couldn't count on it. She had to win.

She risked a glance at her father, saw his face had become deathly pale. She winked at him, as she would have done once before. She would win. Make him proud. Philips might be bigger, but he was slow—all bluster, no skill. He might have longer arms, but she was nimble in a close-quarter match.

The duke made everyone take a large step back, expanding the circle so they had room to move.

"Winston?" Stratford squawked. "What the hell do you think you're doing fighting?"

She ignored him as she and her opponent began to circle, and then Philips lunged at her unusually fast. Winston slipped under his arm and kicked at his knee.

Philips howled, and she danced back on the balls of her feet.

Behind her, the wagering grew fierce, but Philips was on his guard now and came at her directly. He got one brawny arm about her waist and dragged her kicking into his embrace. She fought to prevent him getting an arm about her throat, but he won that battle in the end.

He was no gentleman. He meant to choke her to win.

"Little worm," he hissed into her ear. "You'll see who's the real man now."

The noise of the crowd grew dim, and the cheering faded as her heartbeat grew louder and louder.

While she still had wits, while she still had air in her lungs, she lifted both knees up high to her chin, and then threw them down with as much force as she could muster. The momentum of her toppling weight brought them both down to the ground, but she'd succeeded in loosening Philips' grip on her throat. She dragged in a lungful of air and rolled to her feet again.

Philips was the one who came up spitting earth, and that made her smile. "Who's the real man now," she taunted. "Does anyone know why Philips can be found in the kitchens before everyone else wakes so often? Does anyone besides me think he's looking a little portly lately?"

Philips' face turned a deep shade of red and he lowered his chin, eyes narrowing on her. Win wouldn't say anything to embarrass Cook, but someone was known to be stealing food from the kitchen, and she had thrown the blame squarely on Philips.

"Enough. Enough!" Father cried, unwisely stepping in front of her.

However, Philips had already lunged forward. He could not stop his forward momentum and crashed into Father's back, sending the older man flying into Win and the ground.

She squirmed under their entwined limbs in the deafening silence that followed, and then the duke shouted out, rushing forward to flip her father onto his back and repeatedly calling to him.

But there was no response.

Dazed and unsure of what to do, Winston did not resist the hands that drew her back into the crowd and held her there to watch from a distance. She stared down at her father's still body

—and feared she'd done another terrible thing to him.

But then he spluttered and groaned, clutching at the duke's arm. "Edwin."

Win backed farther away as her replacement went to kneel beside her father, laughing instead of offering him any comforting words.

A well-dressed man rushed to kneel at Father's other side. He grabbed his wrist, checked his eyes, and then started asking a dozen questions, the answers Winston could barely hear.

She felt the pressure of a hand upon her shoulder and looked up. Stratford looked grim as he returned her gaze and squeezed her shoulder even tighter. He reached for her face then, turning it toward him. "You'll need that looked at."

Win pushed his hand away. "I'm fine."

"We'll discuss this matter later," he warned quietly.

Cook rushed over and got between them. "Excuse me, my lord," she muttered. She slapped a raw filet of beef onto Win's face hard enough to make her cry out.

"You were magnificent," Mrs. Derry whispered.

"Indeed," Stratford muttered. "Right up until someone got hurt." He turned on his heel and stalked away.

"Oh dear. I fear you might have lost his good opinion."

"Never mind that. It's you I worry about now.

You must say something about him." She looked over her shoulder to see Philips glowering in her direction. "He's an animal and unfit for a lady's company."

"He is indeed," Mrs. Derry agreed, linking her arm through Winston's, and throwing a haughty glance at Philips. "The kind I shall never trust again near my kitchen."

Winston allowed herself to be dragged to the kitchen, pushed into a chair, and offered ale. She drank it, hoping the pain might lessen if she drank enough of it quickly. A few of the kitchen maids came in, looking at Winston with great curiosity and admiration. Mrs. Derry scolded them for gawking and sent them off to start preparations for breakfast.

"How is the older man?" Winston asked. "Do you think he is hurt very badly?"

"More dazed than anything, I suspect," Mrs. Derry murmured, turning the meat over so the cooler side was on Winston's cheek. "Lord Nash will treat him, never you worry."

She looked at the older woman. "It wasn't right what he was doing to you. I had to stop him."

"I know, lovey," she replied, cupping Winston's jaw. Her thumb dragged over Winston's smooth cheek...and her eyes slowly widened. "No," she whispered.

Winston squirmed in her chair as the woman continued to stroke her smooth skin. But then a smile broke over her face and she began to chortle. "Well, I never! Handed his hat by a slip of..." She nodded. "By a slip of a lad no higher than me."

Winston gulped. Now someone else knew her secret. And that was two too many.

The butler strode into the kitchen next, carrying her satchel. He threw it at her. "You are dismissed, Mr. Winston, without pay. I do not condone fighting among the servants and you have no place here anymore."

"I can't believe Lord Stratford would fire him over such a little scuffle?"

"Philips has been given his marching orders too," Seymour promised. "There are plenty of footmen better suited to holding such an important position."

Winston stood, entirely satisfied with an outcome that would protect all the women of the palace.

She nodded in Cook's general direction and swaggered out of the kitchen, bursting into the fresh air of the kitchen garden. Relief and sadness warred for dominance in her thoughts, however. She was leaving her friend, her lover, and her father, too, without a word of goodbye to either one now. They would never know the truth of this day, and there was nothing she could do about that.

A pair of guests were milling about in the garden, and although she meant to skirt by them quickly, they called out to her to halt. Winston pivoted slowly and saw a woman rushing toward her.

"Are you ready?"

"For what?"

"To make a hasty escape before anyone gets a better look at your face or figure."

She looked the woman over as she extended her hand.

"I'm Mrs. Amity Crawford. The duke's cousin. I've been waiting for you."

"Why?"

The woman drew closer and lowered her voice. "Making love in the outdoors is a particular favorite pastime of ours, too," she murmured, blushing slightly.

Winston closed her eyes. "I wasn't…"

"Oh, you were indeed," Mrs. Crawford corrected, laughing as her husband joined them. "Come along. Time to leave."

Puzzled, Winston followed them to a carriage that had been stopped just outside the walled kitchen garden gate. She reasoned she was leaving anyway and could always ask them to let her out at the end of the long drive.

Mr. Crawford handed his wife inside and then turned to Winston. "I'd offer you the same courtesy if I could."

Winston nodded and scrambled in after him to take a place on the bench seat facing the pair. It was a rich man's carriage, and plush velvet cushions were soft under her fingers.

Mrs. Crawford sat primly, smoothing her skirts and smiling at her. "Are you in very much pain?"

Winston raised her fingers to her jaw and pushed gently. "Not at the moment."

"It could hurt more later," Crawford warned.

"Yes, I imagine so."

Mrs. Crawford caught her eye. "The man you fought with works for my older brother. Would you please tell me what caused you to provoke him?"

Crawford leaned forward. "The better question to ask is, where a woman learned to fight so well," he said, a slow smile spreading over his face. "I was sure you were done for."

"My father taught me," Winston said, deciding she could safely say that much about her past. "Philips was pressuring one of the female servants for things he shouldn't ask for. I didn't like it, so I challenged him."

"That was very brave of you," Mrs. Crawford murmured. "Given everything."

Winston shrugged. "She could not defend herself against the larger man. I could."

"You certainly did. A woman, wearing a valet's disguise," Mrs. Crawford said, grinning. "My, my. Wherever did Cousin Stratford find you?"

"We found each other," Winston answered, lifting her chin.

She noticed they had reached a familiar crossing in the road. To the left was the direction of the inn where she'd met Stratford. To the right was the unknown. "You can let me out here."

"Are you sure leaving is what you really want to do?"

"That was why I came with you."

The pair opposite exchanged a long look, and then the man nodded.

Mrs. Crawford was the one to speak, though. "We have recently made the decision to purchase an estate adjoining Ravenswood, and planned to stay the night as the last owner's, my uncle's, guest. I wonder if you might care to join our household for a little while?"

"Why would you want me after what I did today?"

"The offer of employment is a ruse, of course," Mrs. Crawford promised. "I saw my cousin's face during the fight. I've never seen him so panicked before. There is obviously a close bond between you. A connection that in your current guise he'd not admit to freely before others. It is not right that you should disappear from our society without speaking to him of what might be first." She looked at her husband. "Believe me, running away never silences a yearning heart."

"Indeed not, my love," Mr. Crawford promised, reaching for Mrs. Crawford's hand and kissing the back of it. "A separation satisfied neither one of us."

Winston studied the pair, wishing she knew

more of their love story. Clearly it was an interesting tale indeed.

And she did owe Stratford a goodbye, and she wanted to know that her father suffered no permanent damage, too. She glanced across at Mrs. Crawford and nodded. "I would be pleased to join you for the night, madam."

"Please, call me Amity. What name shall I call you?"

Winston hadn't the first idea how to respond to that question anymore.

Chapter Seventeen

Aston had recognized Win. Stratford followed after the old man and his brothers, who were helping Aston back to the house. Although he looked over his shoulder, he couldn't see Win anymore. The cook would take care of Win, and they'd discuss the consequence of what she'd just done later when they were alone.

Fighting.

Dear God, she could have been seriously hurt. Cousin George's man was a bully and a brute, just like his employer, and Win could have been harmed if she hadn't have moved so fast.

They entered the duke's study via a door left open in the rush to discover what the ruckus was about. Aston had some mud smeared across his brow from where he'd hit the ground, and his face was bright red.

"Does anyone know what they were fighting about?"

"A difference of opinion," the duke said slowly. "I should have put a stop to it."

"Father wouldn't have," Jasper said. "He would have placed a wager and if his choice lost, he'd have dismissed them both."

Aston looked up at the duke. "What will you do?"

"Dismissal for both," Algernon promised.

"I'm not getting rid of my valet," Stratford protested. "Did you see the murder in the other man's eyes?" he complained. "And George was urging him on. Betting on the outcome. He's the only one that should go. I've long suspected trouble between him and other household staff."

"Seymour has said nothing about it."

"I'm sure he's trying to manage the problems without involving you," Nash murmured, holding Aston's wrist, and cautioning everyone to silence while he counted.

"How do you feel?" Stratford asked the older man.

Aston rubbed his neck. "A bit foolish now."

"Don't be. Winston wanted that fight."

Aston frowned. "Winston?"

"My valet. Dane Winston," he said, holding Aston's gaze. "Quite possibly the best last-minute hire I've ever made. Contrary, bossy, but excellent attention to detail. I'd be utterly lost without his help...but I do have to wonder where he learned to box like that."

A ghost of a smile graced Aston's face.

Pride.

The old man was proud of his daughter, and she would know it when Stratford met her later to scold her for scaring him like that. She also ought to know just how afraid the old man had looked while Philips was choking her to death, too.

There was a commotion at the door, and the younger Edwin Aston at last waltzed in unannounced. "Ah, there you are, Father. Recovered from your fall yet?"

Stratford had the urge to punch the imposter right in the nose.

"Not quite. He needs rest," Nash murmured before he slipped from the room around the younger man.

Edwin came closer to get a better look at his supposed father. "You don't look at all banged up, but by all means, retire to your bed if you must."

Aston's face revealed nothing in response to that suggestion. No agreement. No obvious anger, either, that his son would speak down to him in front of others. He seemed comfortable that Edwin cared nothing for his welfare.

When Edwin eventually sauntered away, Stratford was relieved to see the back of him, and he sat himself down across from Aston. He wanted to talk to the old man about Win and discover if he was the threat she feared him to be.

Aston avoided his gaze and sighed. "I should like to see that portrait the duke mentioned to me yesterday. The one of my son."

Stratford stiffened. "I'm afraid it's lost."

"No," Nash said as he strode in at that very moment, carrying a familiar-sized square canvas. "Only badly misplaced."

Stratford shut his eyes briefly as the portrait was shown to Aston.

The man sat forward, his eyes fixed on Win's image. "Bring it closer," he urged.

Nash put it on his knees and let the older man hold it himself.

Stratford sat back, hand over his mouth as the painting was studied at length.

Finally, the old man looked at him. "You did this?"

"Yes. From memory after my visit with Father," he said, brushing some lint from his sleeve to hide his nervousness.

The old man's hand trembled above the canvas, but he did not touch it. "This is very like him. Just as I remember before... Well, when he was younger," Aston concluded lamely, a smile that suggested embarrassment.

"Yes, it was a good likeness."

Aston nodded. He looked at the duke. "Were there any serious injuries suffered during the altercation?"

"Nothing at all serious."

"Good," Aston said, and then inhaled deeply before he let the breath out slowly. "I should like to be present when you give the smaller fellow their marching orders."

The duke frowned. "I think any quarrel between servants can be settled without our interference."

"I insist on being there," Aston repeated.

"After all, their brawl caused me pain and embarrassment."

No one dared mention Aston should not have gotten between them in the first place.

"Actually, the little one has already left," Algernon admitted.

Stratford burst to his feet. "You dismissed my valet away without speaking to me first?"

Algernon gave him a pointed look. "Is there a reason I shouldn't have the final say in what goes on in my own home?"

Stratford gulped and subsided slightly. "No. Of course not, Your Grace."

He risked a glance at Aston, who was now wearing an expression of barely hidden glee. The fellow nodded to him, and his smile widened even more. Was Aston glad his daughter was no longer at the manor to be an embarrassment to him? Or was there something else running through his devious mind now?

"I should like to discuss that other matter," Aston announced. "I believe there is a bargain to be made that benefits us all."

"Oh?" This from the duke.

"Yes, I propose a marriage for one of you to a woman of my choosing." Aston looked around them and his gaze settled on Stratford again. "Should such a marriage happen in, say, one month, I am prepared to halve the debt."

Stratford gasped, along with everyone. "Halve the debt?"

"A not inconsiderable sum, as I'm sure you are aware," Aston stated, smiling slightly at Stratford.

"Out of the question," Algernon replied, bristling. "I will not be buckle to blackmail."

"I should hope not." Aston regarded the duke levelly. "But I did not say it had to be you who tied the knot. No, a duke must be discerning in his choice of duchess and not forced into a poor match. But you have two unwed brothers. Should one of them marry in the time allotted, I will consider forgiving half the debt and expect an invitation to the wedding."

Behind him, Jasper spluttered, but Stratford's mind was in a whirl. If he was the one who married in the next three months, it would only be to Win.

Was that the reason for Aston's smile? Did he know Stratford held his daughter in the highest affection?

"What of the rest of the debt?" Nash asked.

Aston waved the question away. "I'm sure the duke and I can figure that out after the marriage has taken place, but only if there is an expedient marriage to a particular young lady of my choosing."

Stratford heard the stress placed on "lady." Aston's message to him was subtle but clear. Marry Win, wearing a gown, and it would be with his blessing. He'd halve the outstanding debt and be reasonable in his wish for any remaining amount.

"I hardly think—" Algernon began.

Aston's gaze didn't even flicker in the duke's direction as he continued speaking. Aston was waiting for Stratford to decide.

He wet his lips. Torn by indecision. Win would hate to be put in this position as much as he would. "I'll do it. Propose. But there is no guarantee of a wedding so soon," Stratford warned Aston.

Win might not want to marry him. She might not want to wear a gown and be known as a woman. She was stubborn about keeping up her ruse. After all, she'd lived her life that way for an awfully long time because of her mother and father, and knew no other way to go on.

"Be persuasive," Aston suggested and then got to his feet, a little bit unsteady. "I think I will go and lie down for the afternoon. You don't mind if I remain until the wedding, do you?"

"It would be our pleasure," Stratford promised, hoping that could be true. There was a lot Aston had not said about his daughter's existence, but to him, it didn't seem like the man wished her ill. In fact, halving the debt owed to him almost made it seem like he was offering up a dowry for Win.

"Oh, and I will not ask my son to remain for the nuptials," Aston murmured as an aside. "He's only in the way here now."

"Thank you," Stratford replied.

With that, Aston left the room, supported by Nash.

The silence was heavy in his absence.

Jasper was the first to speak. "This isn't right. Why should Stratford have to give up his freedom to marry some chit he's never met?"

Algernon was staring at Stratford, a half-smile hovering on his lips. "He volunteered."

"Everyone could see why," Jasper complained. "Aston thinks to make us dance to his tune just as Father once did."

"Nevertheless, Stratford has come to a gentleman's agreement with Aston, and I'll not have anyone question his decision."

Jasper scowled. "Don't think I'll do the same to reduce Culpepper's debt for you. His daughter is hideous." He stalked away, leaving Stratford alone with the duke.

He sat up straighter as Algernon sat down opposite him.

"You must understand why I dismissed your valet? George will fight me over dismissing his man, too. I must set the right example. Leave no doubt who is in control of Ravenswood."

"I understand." It didn't matter anyway. He would catch up with Win in short order. An hour on horseback would reunite them no doubt. "I'm not angry."

"Good. This is a time to rejoice. With Aston suddenly forgiving half the debt, I can see my way clear to a brighter future. A future that benefits all of us."

"Yes." The cost was still high in other areas,

though. Their inheritances were to be sold off, and they were all still stuck here at Ravenswood Palace for the foreseeable future.

And he had no idea if Aston's secret scheme would work. He'd assumed a great deal about his daughter and Stratford's affection.

Algernon cleared his throat. "I have something that might cheer you up."

"Oh?"

"Yes, an invitation to join our cousin and Crawford at Uncle Henry's for luncheon. A deal has been struck for Crawford to purchase the place. I was supposed to go but I think I am needed here. Aston seems to have mellowed a little too quickly for my comfort. It would be rude for one of us not to attend the luncheon with Uncle Henry. Go in my place and try not to worry about your future marriage. I'm sure everything will work out the way Aston expects it to."

Stratford looked down at his hands. He was dressed well enough to go as he was, without needing another replacement valet's help. But he still had to catch Win. He could go to Uncle Henry's make excuses and give chase. Hopefully, Crawford or Uncle Henry would say nothing against him going.

He drew in a deep breath, longing for things that he'd never wanted before. A woman of his own and the love that might be theirs.

Ravenswood grabbed him by the upper arm suddenly and hauled him upright. "Go. Don't think. Come and see me when you return, too. My carriage is out front, waiting for you."

Stratford nodded and turned for the door. He was going to be a husband soon. He'd never expected that when he'd set out for home.

Algernon followed him all the way to the front entrance. "Oh, and Stratford. Tell the Crawfords I expect them back here for dinner. We'll be having a small celebration. Do ask Uncle Henry to consider joining us, too."

Stratford stumbled down the stairs and into the waiting carriage. He threw himself inside and chewed on his lower lip. Watching the palace grow smaller gave him no comfort, and then caught sight of his destination coming into view and his nervousness increased. The road beyond the estate was flat and empty of win.

Win might be angry about her father trying to make a match between them.

When the carriage stopped before Uncle Henry's house, he saw Mrs. Crawford out in her new garden and headed in her direction first, to give his apologies for having to leave again.

"Mrs. Crawford."

The lady stiffened…and then turned slowly. It was not Mrs. Amity Crawford at all. But another lady.

His heart soared and his steps quickened. "Win?"

The lady dipped a wobbly curtsy, holding out

the sides of her long gown. "Lord Stratford, a pleasure to see you again."

He moved closer for a better view. Because she wore bonnet, he could not even tell Win's hair had been cut so short. It was the first time he'd ever seen her dressed as a woman, and he had to say, ladies' fashions suited her as much as male attire did.

He reached for her hand. "My dear lady," he murmured, then saw her smile slip away.

"They promised not to tell you where I was," she complained. Her eyes darted to the windows of the house, and he looked there, too. The telltale flicker of curtains revealed their meeting had been watched very closely from within.

"They said nothing to me about you being here."

"Would you rather not see me after my vulgar behavior today?"

"No…yes." He caught her chin gently and lifted to look at her face. There was no bruise, and he hoped that might always be the case. "I heard you were dismissed and I was about to give chase. I hoped we might talk about where you might be going next."

She nodded. "I've been invited to live here with the Crawfords."

He threw a scowl over his shoulder at the house. The Crawfords would only have brought Win here at the duke's urging. "No wonder Algernon was so keen for me to come in his place.

I presume my cousin pressured you to change into the dress."

"No. It was I who wanted to. Unfortunately, wanting something isn't always easy."

"What does that mean?"

She linked her arm through his and drew him away from the house. "I have already discovered that living as a woman is not at all as easy as I had first assumed. The worst, of course, is learning not to stride about and throw myself into a chair. I have much more sympathy for the women of your class now. It's only been an hour and there are so many restrictions placed on their behavior that my head already hurts with what I must remember. I never had to deal with any of that growing up."

"Do you regret it? Dressing as a woman, I mean?"

"No. Because it means I will be able to see you again."

"That would please me." He released her hand and put his arm around her. "I shall have to think of a way to thank Amity for bringing you here. I was worried about my best friend running off alone."

She stopped under a tree and turned to look up at him. "Are we friends now?"

"Indeed, we should be." He took up her hand again and held it. "It will make our marriage easier."

She blinked several times. "Marriage?"

"If you want me, I'm yours. It is something I

had thought about even before the events of today."

Winston did not rush to say yes. She nibbled on her lip, looking at him like he'd gone mad. "Stratford, you should know—I am still wearing breeches under this gown, even now. I can't change everything about myself and become a proper bride for you."

"I'm not asking you to change, but I do hope you consider the delight I'll have in taking those breeches off you, again and again, for the rest of our lives, if that is an incentive to say yes," he said, and then took a deep breath. "The other incentive is…I have the unexpected support of your father to marry you."

She drew back, eyes wide. "What?"

He winced. "Your papa has offered to halve the debt owed to him if I were to make an expedient marriage to a lady of his choice."

Win frowned. "Why would you want to marry his choice?"

"He saw you, and he saw the painting, too. He knows there is something between us. I can only assume with us married, he hopes to have the opportunity to see more of you. He told the duke he intends to stay at Ravenswood until the wedding takes place. However, his son will be sent away." He took a deep breath. "So, what do you think? Knowing all that, could you still want to marry someone like me?"

It was a long, painful moment, but Winston

finally smiled. "At least if we are married you'll always be on time."

"That's true." Stratford dropped a kiss on the back of her hand. "Win, my life only got more interesting when I met you, and I'll not let you slip through my fingers ever again."

He kissed her properly then, aware that behind them, somewhere in the house, a newly married couple were cheering him on. He led Win farther away from the house and put his arms around her again. Sharing the news about the celebratory dinner could wait until later that day. After all, it was probably for their wedding announcement, anyway.

Epilogue

Win fumbled with the reticule and fan; an oddly awkward pair of accessories she'd been told she must master to be considered fashionable. Separately, she could manage each well enough. But together, she kept getting tangled up. "Why did I think this would be easy?"

"You could always cry off," a bored voice drawled from behind a nearby set of curtains.

"Stratford?"

"Definitely not," came a curt reply, and the curtains fluttered. The man who emerged from behind them looked like Stratford, sounded a great deal like her betrothed, too, but that is where the similarity ended. Win faced a very unhappy man, judging by his sour expression. "I suppose you're pleased with yourself."

She faced him squarely. "Pleased how, exactly?"

He paused, one hand on his hip as he stared at her. "You bought your way into an important family."

"Ah, you must be Jasper," she murmured, wondering where the devil the man had been for the past month. He had disappeared the day Stratford had offered to marry her, worrying

Stratford and his brothers. She looked for one of them now to come along and make a proper introduction, but they were all alone in the long gallery for the moment. "How do you do, Lord Jasper?"

"Not well," he grumbled. "I've not the stomach for the level of blackmail that you must."

She offered him a tight smile and decided to ignore his ill humor. Stratford had told her that Jasper was all bark and no bite. A scoundrel and rake but kind-hearted to family and small dogs. But he didn't know about her yet since he'd been away for the whole of her engagement to Stratford. "Thank you for being here today. It will mean a lot to your brother."

He raised a finger in her direction. "What would you know about—"

"Jasper," Stratford drawled. "Play nice with my lady, or I'll hang the painting of you that I did when you turned eighteen on the wall here."

Jasper turned his gaze on Stratford. "You wouldn't dare."

"Try me," Stratford warned, strolling closer, but Jasper stalked off in the other direction.

"Sorry about that. I should have told you he arrived this morning without his usual sunny cheer and I've not had a chance to tell him much about you. I also shouldn't have shown him the seating plan for the wedding breakfast. He hates to sit beside the governess."

Win looked toward the doorway her future

brother-in-law had disappeared through and sighed. "He'll warm to me eventually."

"We'll get him drunk," Stratford advised. "He always respects someone who can drink him under the table."

She laughed. "Even women?"

"Especially women." Stratford leaned in and kissed her cheek. "Are you ready for this?"

"Are you?"

"We all have to give up our freedom at some point. You have adapted already, so I must do the same today," he said, glancing down at her new gown with a rueful smile. "I will miss seeing you striding about and bending over in breeches though."

"I'm still wearing them underneath my gown today." Win hated a draft.

"I'll take great pleasure then in undressing you later, my dear," he teased, grinning from ear to ear. They were to stay at Ravenswood tonight before and her lessons in acting the lady would continue for as long as needed.

A throat cleared, and they turned to find Edwin Aston Sr. standing behind them.

"Mr. Aston," Stratford greeted, stepping away from Win. "Good morning, sir."

"It is a good morning for once," he agreed, and his eyes turned to her for a change. "Miss Edwina."

Dane Winston was no more, but a Miss Edwina Stone had recently come to visit with her old friend Mrs. Crawford and fallen in love immediately with Lord Stratford Sweet. They were to be married today. True to his word, Mr. Aston had remained until the wedding day had finally arrived.

"Sir," she said, dipping into a curtsy, pleased she did not wobble in front of him on this most important day.

Despite the month that had passed since Aston had first seen her face again, they'd hardly ever spoken directly to each other. They had been in the same room on countless occasions though. At dinners, and once they'd gone shooting with everyone. Father never asked her any awkward questions about where she'd been or how she'd lived. He never brought up his own past, either. Her mother was never summoned or even mentioned, and the young man who had replaced her had left Ravenswood Palace weeks ago.

Aston would nod and smile when they found themselves in close proximity, and then go his own way again soon after.

"I should like to have a private word with her," Father announced.

"Of course," she answered, glancing at Stratford. "Would you excuse us, my lord?"

Stratford squeezed her fingers. "Don't be long."

"I'll be right there," she promised.

Left alone with her father Win waited

patiently for him to speak. She fumbled with her reticule and fan, then clutched them in one hand.

"It is customary to have a family heirloom to carry into a bride's new life," he told her, glancing at the reticule. "Might I see what you have there?"

Win had nothing of consequence in the reticule and didn't hesitate to hand it over.

Aston admired the rather plain reticule, and then put his hand in his pocket. He pursed his lips as he revealed a thick gold chain and dropped it into the reticule. "This belonged to my mother."

She looked at him steadily. "I want nothing. I expected nothing from you."

"You've done well," he said, smiling quickly. "Very well. Better than I had hoped."

She raised a brow at that remark. "Thank you, but we both know that's not true."

Father had wanted so much for his son, and had been saddled with a daughter who could never reach his dreams. Her replacement seemed to be nothing better than a wastrel.

He cleared his throat and wiped his brow. "I wished happiness for you. The riches of a well-made match with someone you could care for, and who could love you as well. I wished for you to have the partner in life that you deserved above all else."

Win stared at her father steadily. "Even now?"

"Especially now," he promised and glanced around at their surroundings. "You were not prepared for the life you must live. I am proud that my…" He paused, swallowed. "That my daughter has finally found somewhere to belong, and with a gentleman who is not afraid to show how much he cares about her."

Win was deeply touched by his words. It was the first time he'd ever referred to her real gender. She wasn't sure what to say in return. She was as unused to showing him affection as he was to her. "Thank you," she said finally, extending her hand.

After a moment, Father's palm met hers and they shook hands.

As always, Papa's grip was firmer than hers, and then he did something she'd never seen him do before. He raised her gloved hand to his lips and kissed the air above it. "You are just as I remember. You haven't changed at all."

She was pleased about that. She did not want to change in any way beyond the superficial. Her clothing was different now, her hair would be allowed to grow longer, but her habit of cursing had to be severely curtailed in polite company these days. "I should be going before Lord Stratford thinks I've forgotten him."

"Yes. Yes, indeed. We cannot have that," Father agreed. "Might I offer my arm and escort you to the drawing room?"

"I'd like that very much," she promised and curled her arm though his.

They strolled from the long gallery together in silence, up to the door of the drawing room, where two footmen stood waiting at attention.

There, they paused, and together they listened to the low chatter of those few invited wedding guests waiting within. In a few minutes, she would assume yet another identity, but this time it would be one she could keep forever.

When her father attempted to separate himself from her, Win held fast to his arm a moment more. She did not have doubts about marrying Stratford. But she wanted her father by her side. She wanted to allow him the chance of giving her away. "All the way, if you don't mind."

She heard his sharp intake of breath, but then he nodded and started forward again.

Stratford was waiting, his expression revealing his happiness in her decision to let her father have this moment with them. Papa handed her to Stratford and stepped back to take a seat among the family.

Win faced Stratford with a smile on her face.

"You're late," he complained softly, but then he lifted a hand to her cheek and brushed his thumb across her skin. "Another tear?"

"It's nothing. Something got in my eye again."

He glanced beyond her to where her father sat waiting for the ceremony to begin and then leaned close. "I trust this will be the last tear."

"I'm sure it will be." She took his hand. "I have nothing more to regret...but you might."

He frowned at her. "I couldn't."

"You haven't tried to dance with me yet. I like to lead."

"And I like to follow you," he promised. "Besides, who said our life has to be perfect? I'm certainly not, as you well know. And someone has to set a bad example."

She grinned; aware the vicar was ready to commence. But she stole one last long look at her husband and winked at him. "Oh, I definitely agree with you about that."

The End

Next in the Scandalous Bride's series

Love and Other Disasters

A duke's third son is rarely of consequence, a lesson Jasper Sweet has learned well. Anything he covets can quickly be lost to others. Until he finds something, someone, he craves in a way he never has before—the very woman he'd previously reviled. The very woman he'll now fight to keep.

More Regency Romance...

Distinguished Rogues Series
Chills ~ Broken ~ Charity ~ An Accidental Affair
Keepsake ~ An Improper Proposal ~ Reason to
Wed ~ The Trouble with Love ~ Married by
Moonlight ~ Lord of Sin ~ The Duke's Heart ~
Romancing the Earl ~ One Enchanted Christmas
~ Desire by Design ~ His Perfect Bride ~ Pleasures
of the Night ~ Silver Bells ~ Seduced in Secret ~
Yours Until Dawn

Wild Randalls Series
Engaging the Enemy ~ Forsaking the Prize
Guarding the Spoils ~ Hunting the Hero

Saints and Sinners Series
The Duke and I ~ A Gentleman's Vow
An Earl of Her Own ~ The Lady Tamed

Rebel Hearts Series
The Wedding Affair ~ An Affair of Honor
The Christmas Affair ~ An Affair so Right

...and many more

About Heather Boyd

USA Today Bestselling Author Heather Boyd
believes every character she creates deserves their
own happily-ever-after—no matter how much
trouble she puts them through. With that goal in
mind, she writes steamy romances that skirt the
boundaries of propriety to keep readers enthralled
until the wee hours of the morning.

Heather has published over fifty regency romance
novels and shorter works full of daring seductions
and distinguished rogues. She lives north of
Sydney, Australia, with her trio of rogues and pair
of four-legged overlords.

Find out more about Heather at:
Heather-Boyd.com